THE TURNING POINT

Barbara Taylor is on holiday, incognito, at the hotel her company has recently failed to take over. There she meets Jim Farrell, the harassed owner, and his young daughter Leanne. Then, fate intervenes in their lives and undercurrents threaten them. Barbara becomes so involved with the family that telling the truth about herself could shatter her new-found happiness — but eventually, when all is revealed, she can only hope that love will be kind to her.

Books by Phyllis Mallett in the Linford Romance Library:

LOVE IN PERIL

PHYLLIS MALLETT

THE TURNING POINT

Complete and Unabridged

LINFORD
Leicester

First published in Great Britain in 1986

First Linford Edition
published 2013

British Library CIP Data

Mallett, Phyllis.
The turning point. - -
(Linford romance library)
1. Love stories.
2. Large type books.
I. Title II. Series
823.9′2–dc23

ISBN 978–1–4448–1504–7

Published by
F. A. Thorpe (Publishing)
Anstey, Leicestershire

Set by Words & Graphics Ltd.
Anstey, Leicestershire
Printed and bound in Great Britain by
T. J. International Ltd., Padstow, Cornwall

This book is printed on acid-free paper

1

Barbara Taylor sighed in exasperation and reached for the desk telephone. A frown creased her normally smooth forehead as she closed her blue eyes and pressed trembling fingers against them. Her headache was getting worse! What had started as a dull ache was now an agony of throbbing pulses demanding the whole of her attention. It was impossible to think clearly.

'Hello?' Her son's voice sounded at the other end of the line and Barbara struggled to remember why she had called him. Her gaze took in the letter on the desk and she moistened her lips.

'Derek, I have a letter from Jim Farrell of the Crown Hotel, Bilham, in Norfolk. He's calling off the take-over negotiations. What's going on? I gave you the deal to handle and laid down reasonable guidelines. You're always telling me how clever you are and that I ought to give you more responsibility, but you've obviously made a mess of what should have been a straightforward business. No wonder I can't take a holiday!'

'Hold on, Mother!' Derek's voice hardened. 'I was handling it until Adrian decided that he could do better, so you'll have to take it up with him. He seems to think he's the only one with brains around here.'

Barbara winced at the resentment in his voice. Normally she did what she could to keep the peace between Derek and Adrian, but her son was learning the business fast and Adrian, an established partner and fellow director, was jealous of Derek's progress in the company and seemed determined to keep him subordinate in the hierarchy.

'Get hold of Adrian and come to my office.' Barbara hung up before he could protest. Suddenly she was tired of her whole way of life. In the five years since Charles died she'd thrown herself into the family hotel business and made it prosper. They now had four hotels and were in the process of acquiring more, but she was only human and the pace was beginning to tell.

Barbara recognised her need to spread the work-load and she gave both Derek and Adrian the chance to prove their mettle, but Adrian inevitably set himself up against Derek and an impossible situation had evolved. Barbara was in no mood to tolerate their petty squabbles. She was determined to stop the rot before the company suffered further damage.

Barbara was an attractive woman of 40, though her eyes at the moment were clouded with weariness and her blonde hair had lost some of its accustomed lustre. Gazing down from her high office window on the familiar London scene she reached a painful decision. It was obvious that she could not continue to run the business as she had in the past. It was too much for her, and the sooner she got away for a complete break the better.

The telephone rang and she picked up the receiver. 'I told you not to put any more calls through for me, Jenny,' she snapped at her secretary.

'It's not Jenny,' Adrian's voice retorted. 'What's on your mind, Barbie?'

She sighed. Adrian had never missed an opportunity to throw himself at her. At 45 he was still handsome and unattached, but there was something in his personality that left Barbara cold although she had never betrayed her feelings to Adrian.

He was pushy and arrogant and couldn't be trusted to obey even the simplest instructions without first arguing the point. But he had shares in the business and his father and Barbara's father had founded the company of Taylor Baybrooke.

'I told Derek to bring you here,' she retorted.

'I'm busy at the moment.' He was always testing her authority, making life just that little bit more difficult, and, although she usually tolerated his teasing behaviour, this morning she had no inclination to be charitable.

'You're not the only one who is busy,' she answered. 'Please come to my office immediately.'

She slammed the phone down before he could disagree, and sat breathing heavily while anger surged through her. She was being stifled, and had to fight against the almost uncontrollable urge to scream. A knock at the door disturbed her and Derek entered, pausing on the threshold to try and gauge her attitude before committing himself.

Barbara felt her sanity returning. Derek was so like Charles that the sight of him never failed to bring a lump to her throat. She suppressed a sigh. If only Charles had lived!

'You look peeved, Mother.' At 21, Derek was tall, and classically handsome, demonstrating the same acumen that had enabled his father to rise swiftly in the world of business. In her determination to teach him everything as quickly as possible Barbara had pushed herself to the limit. She breathed deeply as she watched him cross to a chair beside her desk.

'I did a lot of the groundwork to secure the Farrell hotel before handing the project over to you,' she responded. 'Now it looks as if my hard work's been wasted, so naturally I'm incensed.'

'It's no good blaming me!' Derek's dark eyes glittered and his lips settled into a thin line. 'I have to take orders from Adrian and he decided to handle this particular deal.'

Barbara pressed unsteady fingertips to her throbbing temples. It was all she could do to maintain her control. She certainly needed a holiday, she thought dully.

'You're not looking at all well, Mother,' Derek observed. 'Why don't you make an appointment to see Dr Johnson and get a tonic?'

'It's not a tonic I need.' She looked up as Adrian entered and came over to the desk, his lithe movements showing the effects of regular tennis and squash. His face was filled with concern but Barbara wasn't fooled. She had realised long ago that he was uncommonly ambitious and concerned only with furthering his own career.

'You're looking a bit under the weather,' Adrian observed, taking a seat beside Derek.

'I have an almost permanent headache these days,' she replied, picking up the letter from Jim Farrell. She held it out accusingly. 'I understand that you've taken over these negotiations, so explain this.'

Silence ensued while Adrian read the letter, and his expression hardened slightly. But when he looked up at her there was a defensive smile on his lips.

'You must have read my notes on the take-over,' Barbara said sternly. 'They outlined a reasonable offer. Why did you take the matter out of Derek's hands without consulting me? If I thought Derek was capable of handling it satisfactorily then why did you interfere?'

'I was merely keeping an eye on him. He is only learning the business after all, and you have more than enough on your plate these days.'

'It's not the first time you've interfered, Adrian, and with results that have been detrimental to the company. Now you'd better contact Jim Farrell without delay and sort this out. And in future don't interfere with Derek. Leave him to make his own mistakes. It's the only way he'll learn anything worth-while. In any case, I'm supervising him. Do I make myself clear?'

In the stony silence that followed, Barbara heard Derek swallow noisily, but her narrowed gaze did not leave Adrian's face. There was a rebellious gleam in his eyes as he stared at her, but she met his gaze unflinchingly. She refused to be thwarted. If Adrian decided to oppose her then she would quit cold and leave them to the whole business.

'Well?' she prompted, massaging her temples as the pain increased.

'Leave this with me,' Adrian said tensely. 'I'll handle it.'

'That much I'll take for granted. Now what about your interference?'

'I will always act for the good of the company.' Adrian spoke testily. 'If I see mistakes being made, then I'll do what I can to correct them.'

'Are you suggesting that I was wrong to give Derek so much responsibility?' Her tone hardened.

'Don't make an issue of it, Mother,' Derek cut in, a warning note in his voice.

'You've been overworking for months and you're paying for it now.' A wheedling note crept into Adrian's voice. 'It's time you took a break. Do you want to be carried out in a state of collapse?'

Barbara compressed her lips against an angry retort and a wave of emotion surged through her breast. Adrian was watching her intently, a half smile upon his lips, and she wondered why he pretended to love her when they both knew he was merely interested in furthering his own career.

She glanced at Derek and saw genuine concern upon his features. The fight went out of her then and her shoulders slumped as she leaned back in her seat.

'You two have been telling me for weeks that I am in need of a holiday,' she said quietly, 'although you each seem determined to make life more difficult for me instead of easing the load. Adrian even thinks he could do my job better than me!

'Well, I'm going to give you the chance to prove it, Adrian. You will take over from me as of this minute. Derek, you know what your duties are around here. See that you do everything as well as you can.'

'What's on your mind now?' Adrian got to his feet, concern upon his face, but Barbara saw satisfaction gleaming in his eyes.

'I'm going to take indefinite leave!' She could see he didn't believe her and when he chuckled and shook his head she reached out for the telephone and rang her home number. When her housekeeper answered the call, she spoke brusquely. 'Mrs Jameson, this is Barbara. Would you pack a couple of cases for me? I shall be going away for an indefinite period. I'll be home in about an hour.'

She hung up before Mrs Jameson could query anything and opened the top drawer of the desk to take out her handbag. She was trembling inwardly and stood up abruptly, wanting to leave before she was tempted to change her mind.

'Where are you going, Mother?' Derek started to move to her side.

'At the moment I don't know.' She shrugged and walked deliberately to the door. 'The fact that I'll be away from this office is the important thing. Now you start running the business, Adrian. You've been praying for the opportunity, so let's see if you can make a success of it.'

'I'll need to know where to contact you,' he said quickly.

'Are you afraid that you won't be able to manage without me at your back?'

Adrian flushed slightly as the barb struck home.

'I'll be in touch eventually,' Barbara relented slightly. 'But I don't want either of you running after me every five minutes!'

Just then the door opened to admit her secretary. 'Mr Tierney is here to see you,' Jenny announced.

'Adrian will see him.' Barbara stepped neatly around the girl and departed with scarcely a backward glance. 'I'm off to find some peace and quiet. Goodbye.'

'But, Mother!' Derek took a step forward, a hand outstretched.

Barbara closed the door firmly behind her and walked away swiftly. Her head was thumping madly and she felt as if her brain would explode. She had to get away before she broke down completely.

Leaving the office, she drove home to the big house on the outskirts of Shepperton. The morning was sunny, the air fresh after her stuffy office, and she sighed with relief as she alighted in front of the Georgian mansion and gazed across the smooth terrace at the trim lawns.

Here was the only place in the world where she could find peace. Charles had brought her here 22 years ago as a young bride. She smiled faintly at the poignant memory, for the last five years had been spent alone, with Charles buried in the small cemetery nearby. Loneliness spread through her mind as she blinked against a sudden rush of tears and fought against hopelessness.

She went into the house, pausing on the threshold to look around the lofty hall. What she needed now was a complete change — the opportunity to submerge her problems in unfamiliar surroundings amongst strangers. Barbara was sensible enough to realise that she must find relief from the dangerous tensions building inside her.

Mrs Jameson, the housekeeper, appeared at the top of the stairs, and came hurrying down when she saw Barbara.

'I've packed the essentials,' she said. 'They're in the two cases by the door.'

'I'll go up and take anything else I might need,' Barbara responded. 'I don't know how long I'll be away, but I'll be in touch. Get Tom to put away the Daimler. Tell him I want to take the red Escort.'

Mrs Jameson went to see the gardener and Barbara went up to her room, wondering where she should go. She thought of the holiday chalet that Charles had bought many years ago, situated near Horning on the Norfolk Broads, and a pang stabbed through her breast. She frowned. She'd not been near the place since Charles died! Perhaps it was time to face up to her memories and move on.

She located the holiday chalet keys in a drawer and popped them into her handbag. Hurriedly packing a few summer frocks Barbara went down to the hall. Through the open door she could see her car waiting at the bottom of the terrace steps.

The phone in the hall shrilled insistently as she passed it and she stopped and picked up the receiver. Adrian's voice spoke at the other end of the line and she hung up without speaking. As she went out to the terrace the phone rang again. Mrs Jameson started towards the door but Barbara gestured determinedly.

'Don't answer that until I've left,' she instructed.

When she drove away she turned north, driving towards Norfolk, for it seemed as good a place as any to start reshaping her life.

2

By the middle of the afternoon Barbara was driving through Norwich. Her headache had receded and she felt easier than she had done for months in spite of walking out on Derek and Adrian.

Slowing on a sharp bend, she saw a sign indicating the village of Bilham just ahead. A frown touched her forehead as she tried to recall why Bilham seemed so familiar. Then she recalled the letter she had received that morning from Jim Farrell concerning the take-over bid and her frown cleared. Farrell's Crown Hotel was in Bilham!

Driving through the village, she spotted the hotel standing back from the road beyond the village green where a cricket match was in progress. Ducks were splashing in a pond nearby. She paused in a lay-by and studied the scene, her heart swelling with pleasure. She felt like a prisoner newly released from jail. After countless years of unrelenting work she found it difficult to contain this vivid sensation of freedom.

She drove along the road to the entrance of the hotel. Her professional curiosity was aroused and she was keen to take a look at the place. It was at the heart of the Broads holiday business, and although she had been given the opportunity to visit it in the earlier stages of their negotiations she had demurred in favour of Adrian, who'd spent several week-ends here. Now she could understand why he had been so enthusiastic about it!

Tall trees shaded the approach, and Barbara drove over to the car park in front of the hotel. There was a space between a car and a motor caravan and she drove into it. But as she braked to a halt, a girl, about eight years old, ran around the caravan and collided with the front of her car. Barbara uttered a gasp and quickly switched off the engine. The child fell in front of her vehicle, although Barbara was sure she'd stopped before the impact. She jumped out quickly, filled with horror.

The girl was lying dazed in front of the car, and Barbara dropped to her knees beside her. An experienced First Aider, she checked and found no broken bones.

Struggling to sit up, the girl started to cry.

'Do you hurt anywhere?' Barbara inquired anxiously.

'I banged my chin on your car,' came the shaken reply. 'And I hurt my chest.'

'Are you on holiday here, dear? Where are your parents? They should know better than to let you play in a busy car park.'

'My mummy's dead.' A defensive note crept into the girl's voice. 'I'm not on holiday. I live here.'

Barbara's eyes softened, and her tone became gentle as she realised that the child was badly shaken. 'Oh!' she said quietly. 'If you live here then why hasn't your father taught you to stay away from cars?'

'He's busy.' The girl dried her eyes. 'This is the high season!' She had dark eyes and an old-fashioned manner. Her brown hair was cut in a straight fringe and shone beautifully.

'What's your name?' Barbara stood up and took hold of the girl's hand. 'We'd better see your father and tell him what happened.'

'Don't tell him!' The girl was instantly aroused. 'He'll be angry and won't let me out to play, and Ruth will make me do odd jobs in the hotel.'

'Who's Ruth?' Barbara walked to the hotel entrance.

'She works here. I don't like her. She's too bossy.'

'You haven't told me your name yet,' Barbara reminded her.

'Leanne Farrell. Who are you? Are you going to stay here?'

'I am on holiday,' Barbara admitted. 'I stayed here once a long time ago, with my husband.'

'My mother was alive a long time ago,' Leanne confided. 'I really don't remember her. She was killed in a coach crash.'

'I'm sorry to hear that!' Barbara was touched by the child's manner. The small hand that held hers was trusting, and a thread of emotion unwound itself in Barbara's mind, reminding her of the daughter she had always wanted. But after Derek was born it had not been possible for her to have another child.

Leanne led her into the lobby. The reception desk was deserted. Barbara glanced around critically. The place was clean enough, but the little touches that made all the difference were absent. There was a bell on the counter and Leanne ran forward and struck it sharply. A woman's figure was visible in the glass-panelled office to the left but she did not respond. Leanne rang the bell again, then came back to Barbara's side, taking her hand once more and holding it tightly. The woman emerged from the office.

'Leanne, if you don't stop ringing that bell I'll send you up to bed with no tea.'

'I rang the bell,' Barbara said quickly, squeezing Leanne's hand, and she was gratified by an answering squeeze from the child.

'Oh!' The receptionist stared. She was medium-sized, probably in her early 30's, and there was a harshness in her manner which suggested a chronic bad temper. Her calculating blue eyes glittered as she studied Barbara for a moment. 'Sign the register, please, if you're booking in,' she said grudgingly. 'Do you want a single or a double room?'

'A single room will do.' Barbara signed the register as Barbara Lennard, her maiden name. She almost stepped on Leanne as she moved back, and the girl took her hand again.

'Will you be staying long?' the receptionist inquired.

'I don't know at the moment.' Barbara disliked the woman's attitude. 'That may depend on the service I get.'

'The service isn't too bad. But you can't get good staff these days. Nobody wants to work unsocial hours.'

'I'll show the lady up to her room,' Leanne offered.

'You run along outside and don't get into mischief,' Ruth warned.

'You're not making a nuisance of yourself, Leanne, are you?' a man's voice demanded, and Barbara glanced over her shoulder to see a tall figure outlined against the late afternoon sun streaming through the door.

'Daddy! Where have you been? I looked everywhere when I came home from school. Ruth wouldn't tell me where you were.' Leanne ran to her father's side and clasped his hand.

Jim Farrell bent over his daughter and ruffled her hair, a tender smile on his lips.

'Sorry I didn't get to the school to meet you, Sugar,' he said softly. 'I had to see the solicitor in Norwich. I'm having trouble selling this place.'

'Aren't we going to move now?' Leanne demanded. She laughed delightedly. 'I'm glad! I don't want to leave my friends.'

'Nothing is settled.' He looked at Barbara and came forward. 'Can I help you?' he inquired.

'I've just booked in,' she responded, looking keenly at him and recalling the contents of his letter, which she had read that morning. She wondered what he would say if he realised who she was. But she was saddened by the situation. It seemed likely that his heart was no longer in the business, and for his sake she hoped that Adrian would complete the take-over as quickly as possible.

'Are you on holiday?' he asked, and there was friendliness in his eyes. He glanced at the receptionist. 'Where's the lady's key, Ruth? Remember first impressions count in this business, and you're the first person the guests see when they arrive.'

Ruth scowled at Barbara and turned

to select a key from a board. She placed it on the counter. 'Number thirteen,' she said, and smiled sweetly.

'Do you have any luggage?' Farrell glanced around. He had broad shoulders and big hands, a six-footer in his early 40's, Barbara surmised critically. His hair was dark and wavy, and rather long at the nape of his neck. His manner was somewhat subdued, as if his spirit was overburdened. She noticed a bleakness in his brown eyes.

'I have three cases in my car. I came in first to see if I could get a room.' She glanced down at Leanne, who was squeezing her hand, and the girl shook her head, as if her warning her not to say anything about the accident. She smiled reassuringly, and Leanne beamed at her.

'I'll see you up to your room,' Farrell said. 'My son is the day porter but he's off on an errand at the moment. Shall we get your luggage?'

'Certainly.' Barbara preceded him to the door, and Leanne deftly collected her room key from the counter. She trailed after Barbara as they went out to the car park to collect her luggage. Then Farrell escorted Barbara up to her room, making light work of her three cases.

When they reached the door of the room Farrell set down the cases and held out his hand to Leanne for the key. 'I see you're making friends with the guests again,' he observed, and glanced apologetically at Barbara. 'Now and again she decides to favour a certain person with her undivided attention,' he explained. 'If she begins to make a nuisance of herself just let me know.'

'I love children,' Barbara replied, smiling at Leanne, who came forward to her side as Farrell unlocked the door.

'But you're on holiday and don't need someone else's kids under your feet.' He carried the cases into the room and deposited them near the bed. 'She is a good girl, and she's keen to help where she can.' He looked closely into Barbara's face then, and she experienced an unfamiliar thrill. 'If there is anything you need then don't hesitate to call,' he continued. 'Whatever kind of holiday you have in mind, we could help with the details.'

'Thank you, but it's a rest I need more than a holiday,' she responded. 'I'm going to take things very quietly, sightseeing and that kind of thing. When my husband was alive we used to holiday almost every year in this part of the country. But he died about five years ago, and this is my first time back since then.'

'I see.' He nodded, and for a moment his face assumed a wistful expression. 'I know how you must be feeling. I lost my wife a few years ago. She was killed in a coach crash. It knocks the ambition out of you when your partner goes unexpectedly.' He sighed. 'But life must go on.'

He departed, taking Leanne with him, and Barbara sighed and relaxed. Going to the window, she looked out across the green. The ducks were quacking as they splashed chaotically on the pond, and the sight of the white-clad figures playing cricket revived memories of days spent with Charles. Charles had figured prominently in her thoughts lately. Perhaps it meant that she was coming to terms with his loss at long last.

* * *

She unpacked, showered and changed her clothes, then felt like a walk. There was time enough tomorrow to visit the chalet. When she did stay there she would have to cater for herself, and at the moment she wanted nothing more than to be waited on hand and foot.

Wearing a white skirt, flowered blouse and sandals, she locked her room and went down to the lobby, depositing the key with a tight-lipped Ruth. Barbara smiled as she walked out of the hotel for Leanne appeared from nowhere and stood smiling up at her. Barbara had to resist the impulse to reach out and ruffle the girl's hair as her father had done.

'Are you going to look around?' Leanne demanded, and there was an unspoken plea in her bubbling voice.

'Yes.' Barbara agreed with an amused smile. 'Are you busy?'

'No. Ruth asked me to help out in the kitchen but it's too hot.'

'You should be enjoying yourself in the sunshine, not working in a hotel kitchen! It's a dangerous place for a youngster.'

'I do odd jobs. I dust and hoover and run errands.'

'Would you like to show me around the village?'

'Oh yes, please!' Leanne's eyes glistened. 'I've lived here all my life. I know where everything is, and all the people.'

'What's the rate of pay for a guide these days?' Barbara couldn't help but be infected by the girl's enthusiasm.

'I don't want any money. I'd just like to go with you.' Leanne was already reaching out for Barbara's hand. 'Come on, I'll show you the riverside. That's the first place most of the new guests want to see.'

'Hadn't we better let your father know where you're going?'

'Oh no!' Leanne shook her head emphatically. 'It'll be all right. I'm a big girl now!'

'I still think we should tell your father,' Barbara insisted. 'It isn't right for a young girl to go off with a stranger.'

They found Jim Farrell in the garage at the rear. He was working on a car engine. Parts were strewn on the floor and he had oil and grease on his hands. Sweat beaded his forehead as he straightened, and a frown appeared on his face when he saw Leanne with Barbara.

'What's she been up to?' he demanded.

Barbara explained and he nodded without hesitation.

'That will be all right,' he said. 'Are you sure you want her to keep you company? I'm always telling her not to go off with anyone without first checking with me.'

'Leanne has kindly agreed to show me around the village,' Barbara explained. 'We'll probably be back in an hour.'

They strolled to the riverside and sat in the shade at a rustic table outside a cafe, sipping ice cold lemonade. Pleasure craft teemed along the river, where swans and ducks existed at their peril.

Leanne continued chattering non-stop, remarking upon everything that came into her agile mind. Barbara listened intently, learning a great deal about everyday life in the village and the hopes and fears of Leanne herself.

'I don't like Ruth,' she confided. 'She's too bossy. And I think she'd like to marry Dad. She wants him to sell the hotel. But I don't want to move.

'A man came from London to talk about us selling. I saw Ruth kissing him! And I didn't like him. He found fault with everything he saw. Poor Dad was upset. Billy said he didn't want to move either.'

'Who's Billy?' Barbara asked.

'My brother. He's working in the hotel, but he doesn't like it. He wants to work in a big hotel in London, and last week he said he'd like to go off and get himself another job.'

'How old is he?'

'Sixteen. He left school at Easter.'

Barbara sighed, aware now of some of the difficulties facing Jim Farrell. He had practically agreed to sell at the reasonable price she had mentioned in the first place. If only Adrian hadn't interfered! He had ruined the negotiations. For a moment she was tempted to call Adrian and order him to resume the take-over along her guidelines, but she resisted the impulse, reluctant for Jim Farrell to discover her true identity.

'I think we should go back to the hotel now, Leanne,' Barbara said eventually, and the girl sprang off the seat and took hold of Barbara's hand.

As they strolled back the way they

had come, Barbara found that she could think about her business life in London quite objectively. The problems seemed to have diminished in importance already and she wished that she had taken a break a lot sooner.

After tea she decided to drive out to the chalet. The knowledge that she would have to visit it lay like a black shadow in her mind. She went down to the lobby, and there was Leanne patrolling like a bird of prey. Her face brightened immediately when she saw Barbara.

'I'd like to take you with me, Leanne,' she said, 'but it might be quite late before I get back and I suspect that you have to go to bed early to be up for school in the morning.'

'I go to bed at eight every evening,' Leanne said, her face falling.

'Never mind. That's one of the penalties of being young. Perhaps you could go into Norwich with me tomorrow afternoon when you get out of school.'

'Oh yes! I'll be home at half past three.'

'Then I'll be waiting for you, and I'll have a word with your father before you get home.'

'Thank you, Mrs Lennard!' Leanne's face was wreathed in smiles. She waved excitedly to a tall youth who appeared through the doorway leading into the kitchen. 'That's my brother, Billy! I told him all about you. He said I shouldn't get too familiar with the guests.'

'And he has a point, I expect,' Barbara responded. She said goodbye and drove carefully out of the car park, keenly aware that Leanne watched her intently until she was out of sight.

* * *

When she got her first glimpse of the Broads Barbara caught her breath sharply, remembering the happy times she had spent here with Charles. But nothing seemed to have changed as she turned into a narrow lane and drove slowly until she reached her chalet.

Leaving the car, she fumbled in her handbag for the door key. The outside of the chalet was freshly painted, for she had arranged for a local estate agency to maintain it. But this was her first visit since Charles died.

Unlocking the door, she pushed it open and paused on the threshold for a few moments. There was a tense feeling in her breast. The air was musty, warm from the trapped heat of the day, and the interior was dim because the curtains were drawn. She stifled a sigh and entered, going around immediately to open all the windows and let in the evening breeze.

She checked that the water was turned on and the electricity supply had not been disconnected. Looking around, she saw familiar objects, and sadness trickled through her. But there was a sense of resolution welling up inside her, like a delicate plant seeking light and warmth to nurture it.

When the atmosphere became too

oppressive she went outside to the boat-house and unlocked the door to look at the big cabin cruiser moored inside. It had been Charles's pride and joy. Its name was painted in golden letters on the bows and the stern, Lady Barbara. It had been a standing joke between them, a reference to George Bernard Shaw's work and to Barbara herself.

The sun had disappeared in crimson glory beyond the horizon and dusk had closed in when she stirred and went back into the chalet. Switching on the lights, she suddenly felt the need for action. The telephone was still connected, and she steeled herself as she put through a call to her home. Mrs Jameson answered.

'Hello, is Derek at home?' Barbara asked.

'No. He went out an hour ago. Can I take a message?'

Barbara smiled. Mrs Jameson didn't hear too well over the telephone and had not recognised her voice. 'No,' she said. 'I'll call again.'

Ringing off, she telephoned Adrian, and there was a frown on her face as she considered him. Leanne had seen him kissing Ruth! So that was the kind of man he was! Always professing love for Barbara herself but playing the field whenever the opportunity arose.

'Hello.' Adrian's voice was curt when he answered.

'It's Barbara,' she said.

'Barbara!' His tone changed. 'Where are you? I've been worried. At one stage I considered calling the police and getting them to trace you.'

'The police! Why? I'm on holiday, and enjoying it immensely, I might add. I'd forgotten what it's like to have time for myself outside of business pressures. However, there is one thing on my mind and I want it settled. What have you done about the Farrell take-over?'

'Nothing yet. I plan to give Farrell a few days to sweat and then make another approach.'

'Adrian, you'd better handle it just as

I advised.' She became angry. 'If I call again and learn that you are still trying to thwart me then there will be trouble.

'Ring Farrell as soon as I hang up. Make any excuses you like but sweeten him and resume the negotiations. When I call you again you'd better be able to report some progress. Is that clear?'

'All right. But where are you? I may need to call you urgently.'

'There's no need for you to know where I am. Just do as I say. Goodbye.'

She dropped the receiver on its rest and sat breathing hard, her eyes bright and her lips compressed. Then she relaxed. One thing was emerging from all of this, she thought grimly. She was learning a great deal about the real Adrian.

She was smiling when she locked the chalet and drove back to the hotel. A sense of well-being was spreading through her mind, a kind of relief that seemed to indicate that she was rising above her problems. Now she could really begin to enjoy her holiday!

3

The next morning Barbara awoke very early and decided to take a quick walk before breakfast. But as she was coming down the stairs she heard a commotion going on in the office. A woman emerged and hurried out of the hotel. Ruth appeared, white-faced and angry. She glared at Barbara and then went to the entrance and called after the departing woman.

A door at the rear of the lobby opened and Jim Farrell appeared, frowning when he saw Ruth. He came forward quickly but paused when he spotted Barbara standing on the bottom stair.

'Good morning, Mrs Lennard,' he greeted. 'You're up bright and early. Going for a walk before breakfast?'

'Yes. It's a lovely morning!' Barbara felt completely refreshed, and the pressures of the previous day were already fading from her mind. 'Oh, before I forget, I've asked Leanne to come with me to Norwich after school, if you agree.''

'That will be fine.' He smiled as he studied her face. 'It's good of you to take an interest in Leanne. I do the best I can for her, but with this place to run it isn't always easy to get off duty when I'd like to. At the moment I'm having trouble keeping the right kind of staff.'

'I know what you mean.' Barbara chuckled. 'I was in this business for a good many years.'

'Really?' He was immediately interested. 'May I ask where?'

'On the south coast generally. My husband was the manager of a hotel and I helped him run it.' She was deliberately vague and he did not press her further.

'So you know all about the vagaries that can beset a hotelier!' He shook his head ruefully. 'My wife was my right hand and I'm still lost without her. It's bad enough not having her around for Leanne, but she was a marvel when it came to running this place.'

Ruth returned from outside, her shoulders heaving as if she had been running. She ignored Barbara and spoke to Farrell.

'We're in trouble,' she said flatly. 'Joan has gone home.'

'Joan?' Farrell was shocked. 'Is she ill?'

'No. She took umbrage at some little remark I made.'

'Oh no!' He heaved a sigh. 'I've warned you about letting your tongue run away with you, Ruth! I'd better go and fetch her.'

'You'll be wasting your time. She won't come back. She was no use, anyway. Never on time and always slacking when she was here.'

'Is there anything I can do to help?' Barbara offered. 'I know what it's like trying to cope with a staff shortage.'

'I couldn't ask you to help.' He spoke worriedly. 'You're a guest.'

'I've been in the business and I know what it's all about,' she reminded.

'Yes, but you're on holiday.' He shook his head helplessly. 'What a mess! I'm tempted to sell out even at the criminal price Taylor Baybrooke are offering.'

Barbara winced at the mention of her company, but she'd made up her mind. 'I'll help out until you can get someone else,' she said firmly. 'Where do I start?'

'The kitchen is through here.' Jim still sounded doubtful. 'Please follow me.'

Barbara hurried after Jim and found his son, Billy, busy at a sink. Jim called to him.

'Billy, this is Mrs Lennard. She's a guest in the hotel but she's offered to help out this morning. We've got problems with Joan.'

'I know!' Billy spoke angrily. 'I heard the row going on between her and Ruth. It's about time you did something about Ruth, Dad. She's killing us off.'

'Never mind about that now. We've

got to get moving before the guests start coming down for breakfast. The service in this place has degenerated as it is. If we let it sink any lower it will disappear altogether.'

'Leave it to us,' Barbara said confidently. 'Billy and I will be able to handle it. Will you show me where everything is, Billy?'

'Certainly, Mrs Lennard. I'd rather work with you than Ruth.'

Barbara soon established a good working relationship with Billy, who proved to be a great help. He smiled a lot, and threw a stream of helpful advice at her. A waitress, Pamela, arrived before breakfast started, and began moving swiftly between the kitchen and the dining room.

Jim appeared finally, smiling, relieved because breakfast had gone off without a hitch. He looked at Barbara's hot, flushed face and nodded slowly.

'I don't know what we'd have done without you,' he said fervently. 'I'll ring the Job Centre and see if I can get some staff. But everyone's been fed and the crisis is over for the time being.'

'I know one guest who hasn't had breakfast,' Barbara said, and saw him frown. 'Me,' she added, and laughed.

'Oh dear!' He shook his head. 'How can I apologise, and how do I repay you for what you've done?'

'Don't worry about it.' Barbara brushed a wisp of damp hair back from her forehead. 'I thoroughly enjoyed myself this morning. I wouldn't mind helping out while you're short-handed. It's therapy to me, working in a kitchen again.'

'I don't know what to say!' Jim shook his head, a frown upon his rugged face. 'But first things first. Go and sit down and we'll have breakfast. I'm about to do my own. Is there anything you particularly fancy? I'll attend to it personally.'

'After all the bacon and eggs I've just cooked I'm rather afraid that I'm beyond that sort of thing now.' Barbara was smiling. 'I'll have some toast and marmalade, that's all.'

'Tea or coffee?'

'Tea, please.' She sighed and removed her overall.

'Thanks Mrs Lennard,' Billy called. 'No-one's ever handled breakfast as well as you. Not even Mother! Are you sure you wouldn't like a regular job here?'

'We'll have to see about that!' Barbara smiled as she departed for the dining room. It was a great relief to sit down and relax. Physically she was tired, but felt a great deal of satisfaction as she picked up a morning paper and scanned the news.

Presently Jim came through with her toast and tea, and she thanked him. He disappeared again, to return moments later with a plate of eggs and bacon.

'Mind if I join you?' he asked, and sat down when she nodded.

They ate in near silence, and Barbara studied him closely, now seeing him as a man for the first time — liking what she saw. When he was not preoccupied by his worries his expression softened and he was very attractive. Pushing aside his plate, he smiled when he met her gaze.

'That's better,' he commented. 'Now I'd like to talk to you before I start engaging more staff. Are you looking for a position? Either semi-permanent or otherwise?'

'I wasn't.' Barbara shook her head slowly. 'But if I can help you then I'll do so. It won't hurt me.'

'That's kind of you.' He smiled gratefully. Barbara liked him instinctively and hoped she could ease his problems, especially where Leanne was concerned.

'But we must come to a financial arrangement,' he went on. 'Personally I'd be quite happy to give you a job in any capacity, judging by your performance in the kitchen this morning.'

'A seasonal job, perhaps,' she said quietly, and added, 'if you're not selling out.'

He was silent for a moment, and then

sighed and shook his head. 'I don't know what to do for the best,' he admitted. 'If I stay here I'm sure I'll go mad. But if I sell out I'll lose a lot of money and make my two children unhappy. Leanne doesn't want to lose her friends, and she's had enough to contend with as it is.

'Unfortunately there's a limit to what I can do. I've tried just about everything, but I don't seem to be able to get it right.'

'What would you do if you sold out?' she pursued. 'Have you given any thought to that?'

He shrugged. 'Quite a lot of thought has gone into it, but I still haven't made up my mind. On the face of it I don't care. It's the children who really count. I know Billy would like to get a job in a bigger hotel, preferably in London, but I've told him that he will need to study several related subjects if he hopes to qualify as something better than a porter.'

'He would need to take some

full-time courses,' Barbara agreed. 'And he should start now.'

'But he can't do much until I make up my mind about the future.' Jim pulled a face. 'I've made a mess of my life and it's beginning to look as if I'm spoiling the few chances my children might have.'

A sullen-faced Ruth appeared in the doorway. Jim glanced around and then shifted his chair.

'Is there something you want, Ruth?' he called.

'There's a phone call for you. Adrian Baybrooke. He wants to talk to you.'

'Excuse me.' Jim got to his feet and hurried out.

So Adrian had finally called, Barbara thought, and this early in the morning! She wondered if there were any special significance in the fact, and wished she could have overheard their conversation. She realised that Ruth was still standing in the doorway, and rose and walked towards the receptionist.

'Are you going to be working here

now?' Ruth demanded.

'I don't know yet. I must admit I'm attracted to the idea of working in a hotel again.' Barbara suspected Ruth hated the thought of her staying, and could not resist the opportunity to make the woman squirm. She could understand why Leanne did not like Ruth and could not help wondering what the woman was up to.

* * *

Going up to her room, she almost bumped into Billy, who was running a vacuum cleaner over the top corridor carpet.

'You're a jack-of-all-trades, Billy,' she commented, and he nodded, grinning shyly.

'Dad says it's a good start to a career in hotel work,' he replied.

'Is that your ambition?' She recalled what Leanne had said about Billy wanting to work in a big hotel in London, and thought of Derek, aware that he was fortunate to have all the advantages in life.

'I don't really know,' he said shortly. 'I wouldn't like to finish up like Dad, not knowing which way to turn.'

'But that's because your mother died, isn't it? You can hardly judge him on what you see now, because that wouldn't be fair.'

'Dad has let things slide. Now he's talking of selling out and becoming a manager in another hotel. But I don't think that would work for him. It would just be a step down the ladder.'

'You could be right.' Barbara nodded. 'You're a perceptive young man, Billy, and you ought to go far. Learn all you can, and don't be afraid of hard work. I liked the way you were working in the kitchen this morning. You've got it in you to do well in this business.'

'Thanks, Mrs Lennard. Thanks a lot. I appreciate your praise. You seem to know what you're talking about. You did very well yourself this morning.'

Barbara chuckled as she turned away.

'That comes with practice,' she explained. 'A lot of practice, Billy.'

Barbara spent a restful day, wandering leisurely around the countryside allowing her mind to recuperate from past traumas. She returned to the hotel at three in the afternoon to prepare for the trip to Norwich, fully expecting Leanne to appear as soon as she arrived home from school.

A knock at the door as she was tidying her hair brought a smile to her face. Leanne already! When she answered the door she found Jim standing there.

'Hello,' he said. 'I just wanted to tell you that Leanne is back and eager to be off. If she hasn't bored you to tears already she's sure to do so in a few days. I can tell her that you're not going to Norwich now, if you'd rather not take her.'

'You'll do no such thing,' Barbara said, horrified by the thought. 'I'm quite looking forward to her company.'

He started to leave, then paused and

glanced at her. Barbara smiled. 'Is there something on your mind?' she asked.

'There's always something on my mind.' He sighed. 'I've spent most of the day trying to employ more staff. I need a chef, a waitress and a couple of cleaners. But the season has started and all the best workers are already employed.

'You managed the kitchen very well this morning and I'd be happy to have you working here. I'm only saying this because you seem to be looking for something to occupy your mind. I get the feeling that you're running away from something or someone.'

'Really?' Barbara nodded. 'Well, I suppose I am in a way. I got myself into such a rut that it's a wonder I didn't become a nervous wreck.'

'So you really don't need a job?' he persisted.

'Financially, no. But I really enjoyed the work this morning. It could save my sanity. If you are serious about employing me then I'd like to accept on a temporary basis. Keep an eye open for someone suitable and I'll fill in until you find a replacement.'

'Thank you. I was hoping you would. You can work any hours that would suit you, breakfast being the most vital time.'

'I'll cover breakfast then, and lunches. Shall I work from six in the morning until two?'

'Perfect. I'll pay you the going rate. You won't get a bill for staying here and all the meals will be free.'

'That's very generous!'

'You're doing me a great favour.' He smiled. 'I'll be in your debt. This is a bad time for me, and really, I don't know which way to turn.'

'Try not to worry too much,' she advised. 'I'm sure it will all work out. A couple of days ago I was worrying myself into a shadow but now I've made a firm decision about my life everything seems to be working out. Decide what you really want to do and then go all out for it.'

'That sounds like a very good piece of advice.' He nodded as he departed. 'I'll bear it in mind.'

* * *

Leanne was waiting patiently when Barbara finally descended the stairs, and Ruth was scowling from behind the reception desk. Barbara took hold of Leanne's hand as they went out to the car.

'How was your school today?' Barbara asked when they were driving towards Norwich.

'I couldn't wait to get out, knowing I was going with you,' came the pert reply.

'Do you like school?'

'It's all right.'

'What would you like to do when you leave school?'

'I'm not sure. I thought I'd work in a hotel like Daddy, but he's going to sell ours and I don't know where we'll go.'

Barbara pricked up her ears, wondering what had transpired during the day. 'Your daddy said yesterday that he might not be selling,' she prompted.

'He got a telephone call today from Adrian. You know, the man in London I don't like. Adrian still wants to buy the hotel, and he's offered Daddy more money.'

'I see.' Barbara was pleased that Adrian now seemed to be following instructions. But it was obvious that Jim had a number of problems. Neither he nor Leanne would be happy with a move at this time. So what was the alternative? Would he roll up his sleeves and make the best of what he had?

'You helped in the kitchen this morning,' Leanne reproved. 'I was looking all over for you when I came down to breakfast, and Ruth wouldn't tell me where you were.'

'Did you know that I'm going to work in the kitchen for a time?' Barbara glanced at the girl, noting her bubbling excitement.

'Are you?' Leanne was amazed. 'But you don't look like a lady who works in a hotel.'

'I've worked around hotels for most of my life.' Barbara chuckled.

'Are you married? You came to the hotel alone.'

'I'm not married now.' Barbara concentrated upon her driving for they were entering the city. 'What would you like to do? I used to come to Norwich quite often some years ago. I'd like to see the sights again. Can you show me around?'

'I can take you to the castle, and the cathedral. I know all the places.'

'Fine. What about parking? There's a lot of traffic about.'

'You'll have to go into a car park.' Leanne was looking around to get her bearings. 'Turn left at that roundabout coming up. I know a place just past the theatre.'

They left the car in a multi-storey car park and joined the throngs of shoppers on the crowded pavements. Leanne held Barbara's hand tightly and talked incessantly as they made their way to the castle. They browsed around, delving into the artefacts of the past. Then Barbara had a coffee and Leanne had an orange juice. Leanne tugged Barbara's hand.

'We can't leave without dropping a penny down the well and making a wish,' she said firmly.

'I remember the well.' Barbara smiled. 'We must make a wish. It's for good luck.'

There was a grating in the floor and lights installed at intervals down the shaft gave them some idea of the depth of the well. Barbara watched while Leanne dropped a two-pence piece through the grating, and the girl's lips moved as she made a wish while listening for the splash which came seconds later.

'Now it's your turn,' Leanne said. 'Make a wish, but keep it secret. If you tell anyone then it won't come true.'

Barbara complied, aware that Leanne

was watching her intently. Entering into the spirit of the moment, she wished that Jim Farrell would be able to solve his problems to the satisfaction of himself and his children.

'Was it a good wish?' Leanne asked eagerly, after the coin had splashed into the water.

'Yes, it was a good wish.' Barbara smiled. 'And I hope it will come true.'

Leanne was somewhat subdued by the sombre atmosphere of the cathedral, but Barbara enjoyed the peacefulness inside the ancient building. When they emerged into the bright sunlight once more Leanne clasped her hand and held it tightly. For a few moments the girl was silent, thoughtful. Then she looked up at Barbara with an inquiring gaze.

'What does God look like?' she asked.

'I don't think anyone really knows. We are all supposed to reflect God, so perhaps he looks a bit like all of us. You have religious education at school, don't you?'

'Yes. I like the Bible stories. It's a pity Jesus isn't on earth now.'

Barbara had to agree, and she was thoughtful as they went into the city centre. 'Would you like something to eat or shall we wait until we get back to the hotel?' she asked, affectionately brushing a wisp of hair from Leanne's face.

'We can eat back at the hotel,' Leanne decided. 'Where would you like to go now?'

'I don't mind. You're the guide, so you should take me around.' She paused and squeezed the girl's hand. 'But before we go anywhere else I'd like to buy you a little keepsake. Have you any idea what you'd like?'

Leanne smiled up at Barbara, slowly shaking her head, a finger to her mouth. 'Thank you,' she said shyly. 'But I don't really know.'

'All right.' Barbara nodded. 'Let's take a look in those shops over there and perhaps you'll see something you'd like.'

They crossed the road to a large store. Leanne walked happily, seeming to blossom under Barbara's attention. After searching through the entire shop, Leanne suddenly darted to a counter and picked up a doll with large blue eyes that said 'Mama' when it was tipped forward.

'This is what I'd like!' she cried excitedly. 'She looked so lonely sitting there, and she can be my friend.'

'So be it!' Barbara said softly. 'She's yours.'

When the assistant tried to take the doll to wrap it Leanne refused to be parted from her toy.

'Oh no!' she said. 'She must see the sights with us.'

Barbara looked down compassionately at Leanne who was hugging the doll protectively to her chest. In her loneliness Leanne had reached out to Barbara and she couldn't fail the child. Jim Farrell, too, needed guidance and she was probably the only person in the right position to help him. Her desire to alleviate his situation did not spring from any sense of loyalty to her own business, but came straight from the heart.

4

It was the middle of the evening when they returned to the hotel, and Leanne was practically asleep in the back of the car, arms entwined around the doll. Barbara stopped in the car park and turned to look at Leanne, whose eyelids were fluttering. A wave of maternal emotion touched Barbara and she reached out and stroked Leanne's cheek.

'Leanne, we're back home,' she said softly.

'I'm sorry it's over,' Leanne said, opening her eyes and sitting up. 'And thank you for my doll. I'll never forget today, and I'll keep Tina for ever.'

Barbara smiled. 'Tina? Is that what you're going to call her?'

'Yes. It's what Daddy used to call Mummy.' Leanne opened the car door.

'Perhaps your Daddy wouldn't want

to be reminded of that,' Barbara suggested gently.

'All right. I'll call her Barbie.' Leanne smiled as Barbara joined her. 'It suits her better because you've got blue eyes too, and I like your name.'

When they entered the lobby Ruth was still at her desk. 'I thought you two weren't coming back!' she exclaimed.

'I wish we hadn't,' Leanne retorted under her breath.

'Your father wants to see you the minute you get in,' Ruth said. 'He's in the kitchen.'

Barbara accompanied Leanne into the kitchen. Billy was frying some chips, and he smiled when he saw them. Jim wasn't there.

'Where's Dad?' Leanne demanded. 'He wants to see me.'

'He'll be back in a moment. Did you have a nice time? I wish I could have gone with you.'

'How many hours a day do you put in here, Billy?' Barbara asked.

'Too many,' he replied quickly, and

then shrugged. 'I don't mind, really. There's nothing else to do around here. I go fishing sometimes, but otherwise there's only the TV to watch.'

A door banged and Jim appeared. He came forward with a smile when he saw Leanne and Barbara.

'Hello,' he greeted. 'You weren't any trouble to Mrs Lennard, were you?' He ruffled Leanne's hair.

'Oh no,' Leanne cried. 'And look what Mrs Lennard bought me!' She held up the doll. 'I've called her Barbie.'

'We thoroughly enjoyed ourselves,' Barbara said, smiling. 'Leanne was the perfect guide. I couldn't have found the sights without her.

Jim's eyes gleamed and he nodded slowly. 'Well,' he said softly. 'So long as she's no trouble.'

'Leanne behaved perfectly,' Barbara reassured Jim.

'Have you had anything to eat?' Jim inquired.

'No,' Leanne answered. 'There wasn't time. We had too much to see.'

'Good.' He nodded. 'I haven't eaten either, so if you'll give me your orders, by the time you've washed up, the meal will be ready.' He spread his hands and almost bowed. 'I'm at your service, ladies.'

'I'd like a salad,' Barbara said. 'What about you, Leanne?'

'I'll have the same as you,' came the immediate reply.

'Three salads then.' Jim winked at the watching Billy. 'I assume that I may eat with you ladies?'

Leanne agreed and he bent and kissed the top of her head.

'All right, Pet. Run up to your room and get cleaned up. Then come down to the dining room. You'll have to make haste because it's getting near your bed-time.'

'It won't matter if I'm late for once, will it?' Leanne pleaded.

Barbara went to her room and freshened up. It was strange to think that she scarcely missed the rush and bustle of London. The solitude of the country only reinforced her hatred of the rat race. In fact, it wouldn't worry her if she never set foot in the city again.

* * *

When she went down to the dining-room Leanne was already there, demurely sipping an orange juice. Barbara joined her, and Jim appeared in the kitchen doorway, waved to them, and then went to collect their meal. He served them with an exaggerated flourish, and Leanne laughed, although she tried to remain serious.

When he joined them with his own meal, the girl paused for a moment and then observed, 'You're a lot happier today, Daddy. Has something happened? Are you going to sell the hotel?'

'I do feel as if some of my problems are shrinking,' he replied, glancing at Barbara. 'As to selling, well, I haven't decided yet. I have to consider the future for you and Billy.'

'Do you think we should move, Mrs Lennard?' Leanne turned an appealing gaze to Barbara.

'I'm afraid I don't know enough of your circumstances to be able to advise you,' Barbara replied. 'I do know it will be very difficult for your father to please everyone concerned, and I expect he will have to compromise. All I can say is that I'm glad I don't have to make such a decision. I think it would be beyond me.'

'I appreciate that observation.' Jim stirred his tea before raising the cup to his lips. His eyes were gentle as he surveyed Barbara over the rim, and she felt a tingle touch her spine between the shoulder blades. It seemed to her that his personality was often submerged by the weight of his responsibilities, and only occasionally did his true self shine through.

Leanne finished the meal with fluttering eyelids. Several times she stifled a yawn, and Jim was watching her closely. Finally he pushed back his chair and went to her side.

'Come on, Sugar! It's time you were in bed. Say good-night to Mrs Lennard, and thank her for taking you out and buying the doll.'

'Thank you, Mrs Lennard, for everything,' Leanne said. 'I enjoyed going to Norwich with you. But I'm tired now, and I have to go to school in the morning.'

'I expect I'll see you tomorrow then.' Barbara smiled as she reached out and touched Leanne's arm. 'Thanks for showing me around. I really enjoyed it.'

Jim picked up Leanne despite her protests, and she dropped her head to his shoulder. He looked at Barbara.

'You're supposed to be on holiday,' he said. 'Have you made any plans at all?'

'None!' She smiled as she shook her head. 'I prefer it like this. All I really need is time to adjust, and I have that now.'

'Would you have a drink with me in the bar later?' he invited.

'I want to get to bed fairly early because I'm due in the kitchen at six in the morning,' she countered with a smile, and saw him wince guiltily. 'But I'll look into the bar in about an hour.'

'Would you like another cup of tea, Barbara?' Pamela, the waitress, came to clear the table.

'No, thank you.' Barbara rose to leave, but paused. 'You work long hours, don't you? Didn't you come on duty at seven-thirty this morning?'

'Yes. I work split shifts. I was off this afternoon. But you were in the kitchen before I arrived. I hear you're going to be working here for the season at least.'

'Only until Jim finds someone to do the job.'

'You've been in the hotel business a long time, I suspect.' Pamela was in her middle twenties, tall and slim, with brown hair and dark eyes. She was wearing a wedding ring.

'All my life, it seems.' Barbara stifled a sigh.

'They need someone like you here.

The place will never be any good while Ruth's in charge. Jim has given her too much responsibility and it's gone to her head. He must manage the hotel himself, again, before it's too late.'

Pamela shook her head. 'There was an excuse for him when his wife was killed, but it's become a bad habit now. What he really needs is someone to shake him out of this apathy. Ruth has been trying to hook him for herself, but she's not his type. He's a sensitive man, really, and all Ruth thinks about is having a good time.'

'Well I'm sure he'll settle down. It just takes some men longer to make adjustments, and he has his children to consider as well as the business.' Barbara smiled and departed.

'See you in the morning,' Pamela called after her.

Barbara waved and went up to her room. She bathed and changed her dress. Sitting at the dressing-table, she took stock of her situation. Did she have the right to interfere in this family's life, after all? Leanne in particular would be hurt when she decided to leave. Perhaps Jim didn't realise how much a growing girl needed a woman's influence. Even so he was making the best of things.

Thoughtfully she made her way down to the lobby. Handing in her key, she left the hotel to make a phone call. There were two public call boxes just outside and she entered one, calling her home and getting Derek immediately. She was relieved, for she needed to talk to him.

'Hello, Derek,' she said cheerfully. 'Have you missed me?'

'Mother! It's good to hear your voice. Adrian said you'd called him. I've been worried about you. I wish you'd let me know where you're staying. I'll respect your wish for secrecy!'

'I'll think about it,' she promised. 'How's business? What is Adrian doing about the take-over, do you know?'

'He hasn't said anything to me about it. And I'd like to stay out of that, if you don't mind. When you do come back you're going to have to put Adrian in his place, Mother.'

'I'm aware of that. Don't worry about a thing. Do you have any problems?'

'Not at the moment. Adrian is so keen to handle everything that I don't have much to do. I could probably take a holiday as well and no-one would miss me.'

'I need you there to keep an eye on things.'

'Of course, and I expect you have instructed someone to keep an eye on me, haven't you?' He chuckled.

'Yes.' Barbara laughed. 'Now don't worry about me. I'm having a marvellous time. I should have taken a holiday a long time ago.'

'Don't come back until you're completely rested.'

'I'm not thinking of coming back for some weeks,' she admitted. 'I'll call you from time to time, so don't worry.'

'It'll be all right so long as you do call!'

'Goodbye then. You'll be hearing from me.'

'Goodbye, Mother. Enjoy yourself.'

She smiled as she hung up. Hurrying back into the hotel, she looked into the bar and saw Jim standing in a corner, chatting to some guests. But he apparently had an eye on the door for he excused himself immediately and came towards her.

'Hello. I was beginning to think you'd stood me up. I saw you going out a short time ago and thought you'd found something better to do.'

'I didn't go far,' she responded with a smile.

'What would you like to drink?' He took her elbow and guided her to a seat.

'A Bailey's, with ice, please.' She settled herself and relaxed, watching him closely as he returned to the bar. He glanced back at her, and she caught herself thinking of Charles. It had been a long time since she'd enjoyed male company. In the past, since Charles' death, she had not been able even to contemplate it, but looking at Jim, she felt that it would be easy to forget the past. She was faintly surprised when she realised that at this precise moment there was nowhere she would rather be than here.

He came back to her, smiling, and set a drink before her. He seemed light-hearted, but she could guess how heavily his problems lay upon him. It was obvious that he loved his children, and had loved his dead wife. Thinking of Leanne conjured up a vivid picture in Barbara's mind. It was uncanny how quickly Leanne had made a place for herself in Barbara's heart.

'You look serious,' Jim commented, setting down his glass. 'Have you left any problems where you've come from?'

'I had only one problem, really, and that was overwork. The minute I walked out I was free.'

'I don't believe anyone can walk out at a moment's notice these days and not be compelled to answer to somebody.' He smiled as she met his gaze. 'It's not that I don't believe you, Mrs — ' He paused. 'May I call you Barbara?'

'Please do.' She nodded. 'We'll be working together as from tomorrow.'

He chuckled. 'Perhaps a new problem for you,' he suggested. 'Where did you say you worked before you came on holiday?' He waited for a reply, and when Barbara remained silent he moistened his lips.

'It's perfectly all right by me if you don't want to talk about your past. I'm curious, naturally, having someone of your ability appear miraculously when I can't get hold of good staff. I'm only concerned that you might have left behind — some unfinished business.'

'Such as?' she countered.

'A husband, for one thing.' He shrugged. 'You wouldn't be the first woman to have run away from her husband.'

'Well, it's nothing like that. I told the

truth when I said my husband died five years ago.'

'I believe you. He was a hotel manager, you said?'

'That's right.' She nodded, sipping her drink, aware that he was watching her closely.

'I imagine you stayed on as manageress after his death?'

'Something like that. And this is my first break since then and I mean to make the most of it.'

'So eventually you'll be going back to where you came from!' He spoke gently, trying to show that he was not interrogating her.

'I don't know. I haven't really thought about it.' She shook her head. 'I hope that doesn't make me sound like a woman of mystery!'

'Well, Ruth has concocted several colourful explanations for your arrival.' He chuckled. 'It's a compulsion with her, speculating about the origins of our guests. She thinks you may have run away from a husband, or killed him and are now in hiding.'

Barbara drew a deep breath. 'Ruth is one of *your* problems,' she said quietly. 'It's none of my business, but that's plain to see.'

'I know.' His face became serious. 'She was only a waitress here when my wife died. But she's a bright girl, and helped a great deal in the early days. I didn't care about the business for a long time and she handled most things.

'Now that I'm better able to cope I've realised that Ruth's methods are bad for business. I know it's my fault for letting things slide, but if I had someone like you to take over as assistant manager I wouldn't hesitate to put Ruth back to waiting on table.'

Barbara set her teeth into her bottom lip. He was not as helpless as she had imagined, and that was a good sign. There was a glint of determination in his eyes that had not been apparent before. Perhaps now he would begin to rise above his troubles.

'I had big plans for this place once,' he went on, toying with his glass. 'But when my wife died my ideas turned to dust. There was a time when I thought I couldn't live without her, but I have a couple of kids relying on me.'

'I know what you mean. I felt the same way five years ago.'

'But you seem to have made a complete recovery while I'm still dragging my feet.' He drank deeply from his glass. 'My Leanne has taken a great liking to you, Barbara. I know she's been missing her mother dreadfully, and she hates Ruth. Not that I blame her! Ruth would love to step into my wife's shoes — not that I'd entertain the idea for one moment.'

'It's so easy to make a mistake,' Barbara observed. 'And one like that could ruin the rest of your life.'

'Another drink?' He had drained his glass, and glanced at hers.

'Please. I usually limit myself to two drinks in an evening.' She leaned back in her seat and watched him crossing to the bar. A warm glow was spreading inside her which did not spring wholly from pleasant surroundings and a relaxing drink.

Jim returned and sat in the seat next to her. She was actually aware of his personal magnetism and recalled that in her past Charles had been the only man to affect her like that. She accepted the drink he placed before her and sipped it to cover the sudden diffidence which overtook her. He chatted desultorily until she had finished and set down her glass. By that time she had recovered her poise.

'I think I'd better say good-night now,' she said. 'I mustn't forget that I have to be up early in the morning.'

'I feel really bad about you turning out for breakfast,' he replied. 'I was in touch with the employment agency today, and hopefully someone suitable will turn up.'

'Don't worry about it,' she assured him. 'I'm enjoying it.' She rose and he got to his feet. 'Good-night, Jim.'

'Good-night, Barbara. See you in the morning.'

* * *

At quarter-to-five the next morning the alarm clock shrilled and Barbara sat up immediately, stifling a yawn and reaching out to silence the offending instrument. She checked the time and then arose, taking a quick shower and dressing before making herself a cup of tea. It was precisely five minutes to six when she walked into the kitchen. Jim was already there, with Billy.

'Morning, Barbara,' Jim greeted, and Billy smiled an acknowledgement. 'You're looking bright on a beautiful morning. Would you like something to eat before we start?'

'A piece of toast, perhaps.' She stifled a yawn. 'Goodness! I haven't been up this early for years!'

'I'll do the toast,' Billy offered.

'And I'll pour the tea.' Jim crossed to the stove. 'Everything else is ready.' He glanced at Barbara. 'Did you sleep well?'

'Like a top! All thanks to the pleasant evening I had.' She smiled.

'You'll have to curb that riotous living!' He chuckled. 'Sit down at the table over there and I'll bring the tea.'

Barbara obeyed, and tried to relax for a moment. Billy brought a plate of toast to the table and Barbara thanked him.

'I've got some early morning teas to take round,' he said. 'One of the waitresses usually comes in early to do it but she can't make it this morning.'

'So you get all the extra work, do you?' Barbara nodded. 'I'll give you a hand if you like.'

'Thanks, but don't bother. I can handle it.' He smiled and moved away as Jim approached with the tea.

'I didn't get much sleep last night,' he said. 'I had too much on my mind. I was impressed by some of the things you said yesterday and now I'm inclined to forget about selling the place and make an effort to get it straight.'

'That sounds like a good idea!' She nodded. 'What have you got to lose except your problems?'

'That's the way I'm looking at it.' His tone was enthusiastic. 'I think I lost sight of all the important things when my wife died. Leanne and Billy should come first, and they'll be happiest here where they belong.'

He shook his head. 'Isn't it strange how the truth remains hidden until someone points it out to you?'

Barbara nodded. 'That's the way I've always found it. All one really needs is a friend with enough commonsense to be able to point it out.'

She thought of Adrian as she spoke, aware that if Jim decided against selling then Adrian would be thoroughly discredited. There was a moral in that, she told herself, and finished her tea and prepared for the morning rush. It was time to go to work!

5

Finishing her second morning in the kitchen, Barbara felt as if she had never been away from hard, physical work. The years melted away as she relaxed and shed all her accumulated tensions.

Leanne aroused latent maternal desires in her breast. The girl's child-like attention was both flattering and diverting, and she and the doll Barbara had bought her were inseparable. As the days passed Barbara and Leanne drew even closer together.

Billy warmed to her, slowly at first, but readily when he realised that she was an expert on hotel work and only too willing to help him. He listened intently to every bit of advice she offered. In fact the only shadow in her life was Ruth, who said little but managed to convey her envy and jealousy by manner, expression and glance.

But it was Jim himself who brought about the greatest change in Barbara's life. As the days slipped by a fragile relationship grew up between them. He was touchingly appreciative of her efforts to help him and they met most evenings in the bar where Barbara learned a great deal about him and liked the image that emerged. But deeper emotions were rising to the surface and as the second week at the hotel ran its course, Barbara realised that she was greatly attracted to him.

On Wednesday morning of the second week the breakfast rush was almost over by eight-thirty and Billy began clearing up. Leanne had left for school and Barbara prepared breakfast for herself, Billy and Jim.

'You've got this job down to a fine art, Barbara,' Pamela commented. 'Is there anything you can't do in a hotel?'

'I've done just about everything in my time,' Barbara agreed. Just then, Jim came for his breakfast, followed closely by Billy, and they sat at the table and relaxed.

'Another uneventful breakfast,' Jim remarked, eating bacon and eggs. 'If you stay with us much longer, Barbara, you're going to spoil us for any other cook. We've never had it so good, have we, Billy?'

'Once we did,' Billy replied seriously, and Barbara threw a searching glance at him. His face was set, his eyes narrowed. 'When Mother ran things,' he added.

'Ah yes!' Jim nodded, and there was a rueful smile on his lips. 'It's nice to remember the good times, Billy, but we can't live in the past, you know. Life is for the living. What's past is dead, and we have to learn to accept that.'

'You didn't always think like that,' Billy observed, raising a cup to his lips.

'You're right.' Jim nodded. 'In fact it wasn't until this past week that I've come to realise what a fool I've been. But that's behind me now and I'm looking to the future.' He looked round when Ruth called to him from the doorway. 'What is it, Ruth?'

'Telephone for you!'

'Who is it?'

'Adrian Baybrooke. He says it's important.'

Jim started to rise, glanced at Barbara, and then sank back into his seat. 'Just take his number and tell him I'll call back later. I may not be selling, after all.'

'You should talk to him now,' Ruth insisted. 'You shouldn't listen to other people when it's your life that's got to be settled. If you're not careful Taylor Baybrooke will withdraw their offer and look for another property!'

'Please do as I say!' Jim retorted. 'I know what I'm doing.'

Ruth flounced out and Jim resumed eating his breakfast. He glanced at Barbara, then looked at his son.

'You're not happy here, are you, Billy?' he asked. He spoke to Barbara without waiting for Billy to reply. 'I have a problem with my children, you see,' he said quietly. 'Billy doesn't like working here and Leanne doesn't want to leave. So how do I please both of them?'

'It's not that I don't like living here, Dad,' Billy said quickly. 'But if I'm going to make anything of myself I'll have to get a post in a first class hotel.' He looked at Barbara, his eyes showing that he was troubled. 'You say you've been in the business all your life, Barbara. Can you put me right on what to do? Perhaps you know of a good hotel where I might get a start!'

'Qualifications are vital these days. But if you are serious about working in a first class hotel, and your father is agreeable, then I might be able to put in a word for you here and there.' She smiled disarmingly. 'I do have some influence in certain areas.'

'What do you think, Dad?' Billy gazed steadily at his father, and Jim drank some tea before replying.

'I'd never stand in your way, Billy, if it's what you really want.'

'Thanks.' Billy nodded. There was determination in his expression, and he smiled when he met Barbara's gaze. 'If you could find me a suitable place I'd be very grateful,' he said.

'I'll make a few phone calls,' Barbara promised. 'Leave it with me.'

Billy nodded and left the table. Jim sighed and drained his cup. When he set it down he looked squarely at Barbara.

'That lad has grown up and I hadn't realised it,' he mused. 'It makes me feel old! Do you have any family, Barbara?'

'A son, Derek. He's twenty-one and in the hotel business.'

'Families do tend to stick in the business once they get started,' he agreed. 'But what will become of Leanne I don't know. She seems to be made of different stuff.'

'She's very young yet. Give her a chance to grow up.' Barbara started to rise, wanting to get back to work.

'She hasn't had such a good start so far,' Jim went on. 'No mother, and I've been too occupied with my own misery to care properly for her.' He scratched his chin. 'I must start taking her out more. Since you've been here you've made me ashamed, taking such an interest in Leanne.' He paused and drew a deep breath. 'Do you have anything planned for this evening?' he asked.

'No.' Barbara shook her head. 'Do you want me to work?'

'Good Lord no! I've been promising to take Leanne to the funfair at Yarmouth, and I know she'd enjoy it all the more if you came along.'

'It sounds like fun,' Barbara said. She nodded. 'All right. Count me in.'

'Good.' He smiled. 'I always seem to be asking you favours. At this rate I'm never going to be out of your debt.'

'Don't worry.' She smiled. 'I've got a good deal going here and I know it.'

He chuckled, and Barbara moved away to resume working as he departed.

* * *

Part-time kitchen help turned up every morning in the formidable shape of Mrs Moss, a substantial lady in her middle fifties whose bellowing laugh constantly echoed through the lower floor of the hotel. She always greeted Barbara like a long-lost sister while eyeing Barbara's slim figure with a certain amount of good-natured envy.

'How do you manage to stay like that?' she demanded when she blocked the kitchen doorway with her bulk. 'I've been on a diet practically nonstop since I was twenty, and just look at me! I weigh thirteen stones. My husband only weighs eleven and a half!' She subsided into a peal of laughter.

'You've been here nearly two weeks now, haven't you? It's showing already. I said when I first saw you that you were exactly right for this place. You've shaken Jim up, good and proper. What he ought to do is sack Ruth and put you in her job.'

'I'm only here temporarily, Mrs Moss,' Barbara cautioned, smiling, for it was impossible to accept the woman with anything but good humour.

'I came here temporarily ten years ago! The place takes hold of you! But you look to be a good, caring woman, and Leanne has changed out of all recognition since you began taking her in hand!'

Eventually, Barbara disentangled herself from Mrs Moss, who went into battle against the vegetables, while Barbara herself continued with the menial tasks around the kitchen. Billy arrived later. He had been working hard and was hot, his face flushed.

'Would you like a cold drink, Billy?' Barbara asked.

'Yes, please.' He heaved a long sigh and nodded. 'It's really hot today, isn't it?'

'Flaming June,' Barbara responded.

'Ruth has been prying into your affairs,' Billy announced after he had slaked his thirst. 'She's been trying to pump me, but I told her I don't know anything about you, and I wouldn't tell her even if I did. I don't like talking about people behind their backs, but I think you should be warned.'

'Thank you, Billy.' Barbara smiled. 'But I think I know the kind of woman Ruth is, and I don't have anything to worry about because I haven't done anything wrong.'

'I know that.' He nodded. 'And I've seen the way you've been setting Dad right. I've been trying to do that for a long time. I hope you're going to stay with us. We couldn't do any better than you.'

'It's kind of you to say so.' Barbara warmed to him, and determined to do what she could about his future.

He finished his drink and washed the glass, and, looking at him, Barbara fancied that there was something else on his mind. She placed a hand upon his shoulder as he turned to leave the kitchen.

'If there's something else you'd like to talk about then now is the time,' she said quietly.

He glanced around before speaking. Mrs Moss was at the other end of the kitchen, washing a table and singing at the top of her considerable voice. Barbara saw him compress his lips, and thought he looked embarrassed.

'There is something,' he said at length. 'I heard Dad ask you to go with him and Leanne to Yarmouth this evening. I'd like to come with you but I don't fancy asking Dad. But if you suggested I go, he might ask me.'

Barbara nodded. 'All right. Leave it to me,' she said, and he grinned and departed hurriedly.

Half an hour later Jim popped into the kitchen. He was in shirt sleeves and looked a bit harassed, but he smiled as he paused at Barbara's elbow.

'I thought you'd like to know that for the first time in many weeks I've had compliments about the breakfasts.'

'We'll certainly have to try to maintain this higher standard,' she replied with a smile, and his eyes twinkled. 'Oh, and about this evening,' she continued, and saw a frown across his face.

'You've changed your mind about going?' he asked quickly.

'No. I was wondering if you've asked Billy to go along as well.'

'Billy?' He shook his head slowly. 'I'm sure he wouldn't want to go. He'd regard that sort of thing as kid's stuff.'

'I'd ask him if I were you.' Barbara did not take her eyes from his face. 'I have the feeling that he might jump at the chance, and at the moment it's all work and no play for him.'

'I never thought of that!' He nodded slowly. 'What I like about you is your thoughtfulness, you don't seem to miss a thing. But is it your intuition at work with Billy?'

'You could call it that.' She nodded, and gazed speculatively after him as he departed.

'He's a good man,' Mrs Moss boomed across the kitchen. 'And what he needs is a good woman to take his mind off his troubles.' She looked meaningfully at Barbara.

Barbara couldn't help but be amused. Mrs Moss took no pains to conceal her opinions. A few moments later Jim reappeared looking puzzled.

'Barbara,' he called, and she looked up. 'You were right about Billy. I'd never have believed he'd want to go to the seaside. I thought I knew my boy.'

'Can you spare him from his duties here?'

'Of course. We have a night porter. Billy just fills in during the day. In fact he and I share the porter's duties between us. I'm teaching him the job and this is the best way to do it.'

'What about cooking? Does he do any here?'

'He's quite a good cook. He's got the knack.' Jim's eyes gleamed. 'The boy could go far.' He paused. 'Did you mean it when you said you'd talk to some contacts on his behalf?'

'Of course! You don't think I'd say such a thing if it weren't true, do you?'

'No. You're certainly not that kind of

woman. In fact I'm wondering just what you are.' His tone was friendly. 'You appeared from nowhere! And you have probably forgotten more about this business than I'll ever know.'

'Thank you.' Barbara smiled, quite pleased. 'I must admit that if there is something I do know really well it's the hotel business.'

'That's plain to see. But if you've been in the business most of your life then it's surprising that our paths haven't crossed before this. Would you mind telling me where you've worked in the past?'

'There's no mystery about me,' she protested, shaking her head as she avoided his question.

'But you're not going to tell me anything!' He shook his head, and then shrugged. 'You are a mystery, and it intrigues me. But I'm not going to question you. I'll be selfish and hang on to you as long as I can. I just hope no-one's pining for you.'

'Sheer hard work drove me away

from home, my problems weren't of the emotional kind,' Barbara explained. 'Now, after a breathing space, I can see all too clearly that I was right to come away, even as I did.'

She smiled and turned away but he came after her, placing a hand upon her arm.

'I'm wondering if we have any mutual friends in the business,' he said.

'I'd rather not pursue it, Jim!' She looked into his eyes. 'I'm here to forget my recent past, and I'll work for you until you can get someone to fit in. As my employer you do have certain rights, and I admit that I descended upon you out of the blue. But you can see that my work is all right, so why don't you leave it at that?'

'Sorry if it looks like I'm prying,' he apologised. 'But I'm just curious, that's all. You don't have any rough edges like most of the women who wait or clean in these places. They're the salt of the earth, but you can tell they've been around. You, on the other hand, seem out of place, yet you do the work better than most. That is what intrigues me.'

'One day I may fill you in with some of the details,' she said, suppressing the urge to do so immediately. 'But right now I'd better get on with my work or you'll be complaining at the end of the morning.'

He nodded. 'We'll be ready to leave at about four this afternoon,' he said, and his tone was eager.

'I'll be ready,' she promised . . .

* * *

At two she went off duty, hot and tired. But passing through the lobby, she was startled by the sound of an ominously-familiar voice and a thrill of horror speared through her as she recognised it. Adrian! Then she saw his tall figure standing in the entrance, and turned and fled to the stairs. As she hurried up the steps still glancing backwards, Ruth emerged from the office and made straight for Adrian.

Barbara was breathless when she reached her room, and locking the door sank down upon the foot of her bed. That had been close! But what was Adrian doing here? Since the first two days of her arrival there'd been no more talk of selling. So why was Adrian suddenly concerned enough to make a trip all the way from London?

Whatever the reason, he was here in the flesh, and if he saw her there would be trouble. She pictured Jim's face, and her heart felt like stone as she imagined what he would say if he discovered her true identity. Then there was Leanne! Barbara clenched her fists tightly feeling like a trapped animal, for she could not walk openly around the hotel with Adrian in the building!

She showered and donned clean clothes, then lay upon her bed to rest. She dozed restlessly, and woke with a start at quarter to four! Not wishing to be late she began to rush around in uncharacteristic haste, and when she was ready she paused and looked around the little room. Now what? She sighed heavily. Damn Adrian! Why had he come here at this time?

Moving to the window, she tried to see the cars parked below, but Adrian's car was not in sight, and she had no way of knowing if he was still here. She paced the floor for several moments, until an idea occurred to her, and then she unlocked her door and went out into the corridor, looking around guiltily, fearing that at any moment Adrian's voice would call out to her. She descended the back stairs and left the hotel by the rear exit.

Hardly daring to look back she hurried to a public call box and phoned her office in London, asking for Derek. A sigh of relief escaped her when he came on the line.

'Mother! How nice to hear from you! How are you getting along? Enjoying yourself?'

'Yes, thank you, Derek. But I'm concerned about the Farrell take-over that Adrian is handling. I've just tried to get him but I understand that he's not in the office today.'

'He was here first thing in the morning and he asked if I had heard from you. Do you want me to check?'

'Please. I'll hang on.' She took some coins from her bag while she waited.

Presently Derek came back to her. 'You're right,' he said. 'Adrian is out for the rest of the day. He's gone to Norfolk to see Jim Farrell personally. I think Adrian is making a bit of a mess of this business now.' He chuckled.

'It may seem amusing to you, and probably Adrian deserves it, but I spent a lot of time and energy on that project.' Barbara sounded angrier than she felt. 'I'll hang on while you call Adrian in Norfolk and get the latest information from him. Better still, I'll hang up and call again in about five minutes. Don't let Adrian put you off. I want to know exactly what's happening.'

'Fine. Five minutes then.' They both hung up and Barbara moved to a nearby seat, glancing at her watch. The time passed slowly, but exactly five minutes later she called Derek again. While she was waiting for a reply she looked across the green and was delighted to see Adrian's car leaving the hotel car park. A moment later he passed her call box, and drove swiftly along the Norwich road. Barbara hoped that would be the last she saw of him.

'Hello, Mother.' Derek's voice sounded in her ear. 'I've been in touch with Farrell's hotel in Norfolk and they say that Adrian has just left. He's on his way back to London.'

'Thank you,' she said. 'I'll probably call you again tomorrow, Derek.' She glanced at her watch. 'I have to go now. I'm taking a trip this evening.'

'All right. Have a nice time.'

'You can tell Adrian that I called.' She wanted him to squirm a little. 'Goodbye!'

Ringing off, she walked quickly across the green to the hotel, and found Leanne standing in the entrance, clasping the doll to her breast and looking around expectantly. When the girl spotted Barbara her eyes widened and a big smile came to her face. She came running forward, and Barbara felt her heart lift as she held out a welcoming hand.

'I went up to your room but you weren't there,' Leanne said in an excited rush. 'And Daddy told me you are going with us this evening. You haven't changed your mind, have you?'

'No. I had some business to attend to, that's all.' Barbara experienced a rush of emotion as Leanne clasped her hand. 'Are you pleased about this evening?'

'Ever so much! Daddy promised to take me a long time ago, and now we're really going!'

'Billy is coming too.' Barbara was pleased. 'We'll have a fine old time!'

Barbara was thinking of Jim as she spoke, delighted at the thought of spending an entire evening in his company. But she did not stop to question her feelings. She was on holiday and meant to make the most of it.

6

It turned out to be a memorable evening. They travelled in Jim's car to the holiday resort and parked beside the big funfair on the seafront. Billy accompanied Leanne on most of the rides while Barbara stood with Jim and watched. However Jim insisted that they should all go on the Roller Coaster and they were whirled around the track at breakneck speed. Leanne sat with Barbara, screaming as they sped into the steep dips and gasping breathlessly as they raced up the almost vertical slopes. Barbara had one arm around Leanne and clung tightly to the rail inside the car with the other. When the ride was over Leanne begged to go around again, but Jim lifted her out of the car and they continued their tour of the fun fair.

Later, when Jim announced that it

was almost time to leave Barbara was reluctant to break the spell. It had been a joyful evening for all of them. The excitement of mixing with holiday-makers and the exhilaration of the rides had dissolved any remaining barriers between them.

This small family were no longer strangers to Barbara. Leanne clung to her, turned to her every other moment, and clasped her hand whenever she was not with Billy on another new ride. Jim and Billy seemed bent on taking their lives into their hands when they tried one of the latest rides which sent cars looping and whirling around a narrow track. Leanne and Barbara looked on giggling at their pale faces as Jim and Billy whizzed past.

Afterwards they devoured fish and chips in a small restaurant near the funfair. Leanne was gazing around, her dark eyes gleaming with pleasure. Billy was joking with Jim, who seemed to be a completely different person away from the hotel. From time to time he glanced at her, as if to reassure himself that she was content. When they finally made their way back to the car he slid a hand under her elbow. Leanne and Billy were walking hand in hand ahead of them.

'Thanks, Barbara,' Jim said softly. 'It was great fun, and although those two would have enjoyed it under any circumstance, it was wonderful to have you with us. Leanne especially thrives in your company.

'If you weren't too bored by the proceedings I'd like to do the whole thing again some other time before the season ends.' He paused and frowned. 'Unless you're planning to leave us in the near future?'

'I'll let you know in good time when I do decide to leave,' she promised, 'but the way I'm feeling at the moment, it won't be very soon.'

'I'm glad to hear that!' He squeezed her arm gently and Barbara thrilled to his touch.

On the drive back to the hotel,

Barbara sat in the back of the car with Leanne while Billy sat in front beside his father. At first Leanne chattered about the evening's pleasures, her head resting against Barbara's arm, but as they sped out into the country, leaving behind the bright lights and music of the resort, the girl's head became heavier and dropped lower, until Barbara eased Leanne around and cradled her head in a more comfortable position. Leanne fell asleep immediately, worn out by the unaccustomed excitement.

'It's gone nine,' Jim commented at length, glancing back at his sleeping daughter. His tone was gentle. 'And it's way past Leanne's bed-time. But it won't hurt her to have a treat now and again.'

'I'd love to spend some time out on the Broads in a boat,' Billy said.

'So would I!' Jim agreed.

'Would you really?' Billy sounded surprised. 'Then why haven't we ever gone out on the water?'

'Because you can't always hire a boat at this time of the year. And Leanne has always been too young before. It's dangerous out there, as many holiday-makers have discovered to their cost. But if Barbara would agree to come with us I'll try to hire a cruiser for a day.'

'I have a cabin cruiser at Horning,' Barbara said automatically, too drowsy to guard her tongue. Struggling upright after her rash words she disturbed Leanne, who wriggled and then snuggled closer.

'You have a cruiser?' Jim repeated.

Barbara bit her lip for a moment wondering guiltily what Jim would make of her revelation. Billy turned his head, studied her shadowed face, and then asked, 'Can we go out in the boat on Sunday? It's my day off.'

'I don't know if it will float now,' Barbara hedged, wishing she hadn't spoken. 'It hasn't been out of the boathouse in five years, I'm sure.'

'I'd be happy to take a look at it,' Jim offered.

'Thank you!' Barbara decided to be casual. 'If it's sea-worthy we can take a trip on the Broads.'

The subject was dropped then, until they were almost back at the hotel. Then Billy, who had evidently been thinking about the boat, said quickly, 'I know who would look at the boat before Sunday.'

'Who?' Jim demanded.

'Ruth's father. He works in a boatyard, and he owes us a favour.'

'I don't know about that!' Jim sounded doubtful. 'I'd like to steer clear of the Carters. They're a strange family.'

'Does that mean you'll be getting rid of Ruth?' Billy asked hopefully.

'Ah! That won't be so easy. She does her job despite all the complaints against her.' Jim brought the car to a halt in front of the main entrance to the hotel and Billy slid out of his seat instantly and darted away.

Barbara opened her door and helped a sleepy Leanne from her seat. The child clung to her as they walked into the hotel with Jim following closely.

'Straight up to bed, Leanne,' Jim instructed.

'Would you like me to come too?' Barbara asked, and Leanne nodded.

'I'll see you in the bar afterwards, if you'd care for a drink,' Jim offered, and Barbara threw him a glance and nodded.

As she accompanied Leanne up the stairs Ruth appeared in the doorway leading into the bar, and there was a malicious glitter in her eyes when she saw Barbara holding Leanne's hand.

'Jim, there have been a couple of phone calls for you this evening,' she called. 'I wrote the details on your desk pad.'

'Thanks.' Jim bent to kiss Leanne and then went along to his office. Barbara heard his door close as she ascended the stairs.

'I had a lovely evening,' Leanne said sleepily as she was preparing for bed. She stifled a yawn and reached for her doll. 'I've got lots to tell you in the morning,' she whispered to the doll.

'I enjoyed myself too!' Barbara said cheerfully. 'It made quite a change. I hope we can go again.'

'It's the first time Dad has taken us out for such a long time,' Leanne confided, wistfully. 'I think it's because you came with us. If you ask him to take us out again he'll do it. He listens to you, but he won't listen to me or Billy.'

'In that case I'll be sure to mention it soon,' Barbara promised. 'Jump into bed if you're ready. You've got to be up early in the morning for school.'

Leanne climbed into bed and settled the doll under the covers. 'Good-night.' She paused and blinked sleepily. 'I don't like calling you Mrs Lennard. What can I call you?'

'My friends call me Barbie!' Barbara smiled.

'Can I call you Barbie?' Leanne's eyes glistened. 'I'd like that. It would mean we are friends.'

'You and I are very good friends,

Leanne,' Barbara said firmly.

'Thank you, Barbie.' Leanne closed her eyes contentedly, then opened them and smiled, instinctively thrusting her arms around Barbara's neck and kissing her cheek. 'Thank you for everything!' she said slowly, snuggling down.

'Good-night and God bless!' Barbara turned away, her breast constricted with emotion. Her eyes were moist as she went to her own room.

When she went down to the bar later she saw Jim standing in a corner with Ruth and an older man. Reluctant to approach them, she paused in the doorway but Jim soon spotted her and came straight to her side.

'Come and meet Ruth's father,' he said. 'There's nothing he doesn't know about boats. He's been building them for forty years. He'll test yours for you, and see that you get a good price for it if you want to sell.'

'If Billy is really interested in boats then I won't sell,' Barbara said. 'We could use it.'

Jim glanced at her quizzically. 'It costs a lot of money to run a boat these days.'

'I don't mind.' She smiled. 'Can we all get off duty on Sunday?'

'I think it could be arranged. I'm seeing some job hunters tomorrow. That's why I've asked you to come down for a drink this evening. I need to talk business before I see anyone else.'

'Fine.' She greeted Ruth as they walked to the corner, and shook hands with the girl's father when they were introduced.

'Barbara, I want you to meet Tom Carter,' Jim said. 'Tom, this is Mrs Lennard.'

'How'd you do?' Carter was a big man, broad and well-muscled despite his age. He had to be in his late fifties at least, Barbara assumed.

'There were some Lennards who lived in the Manor House over Styleham way just after the war. The man was high up in the RAF. Are you related to them?' Tom Carter inquired.

'No.' Barbara shook her head, hating the lie. She and her parents had lived by the Broads when she was young. But she could not admit that in case Tom Carter should discover who she really was now.

'There was a baby girl used to play by the water's edge when I was a boatman in those days,' the old man continued in a penetrating voice. 'She'd be about your age now, if she didn't fall in and get drowned. The times I used to warn her parents, but they didn't see any danger.'

'It wasn't me,' Barbara said gently. 'I was born in Scotland!' She had no other choice except to lie, aware that Ruth was watching her intently, although the receptionist did not join in the conversation.

'Young Billy came after me,' Carter went on. 'Said something about you having a boat that has been laid up five years. Would that be the Lady Barbara in Avery Staithe over by Horning?'

'Yes.' Barbara became tense, but

made an effort to speak calmly. 'How would you know that?'

'I heard about it from Bob Milton, who works in an estate agent's over in Horning. They look after the chalet there.'

Barbara expected him to go on and mention her real name, but the moment passed without disclosure and she sighed with relief.

'It's my chalet,' she said with a smile, forcing herself to remain casual. 'My husband died five years ago and this is the first time I've come near the place.'

'If you've got a chalet near Horning then why are you staying here?' Ruth demanded. 'And more to the point, if you can afford a chalet and a cabin cruiser then why are you working in the hotel kitchen?'

'Purely through choice.' Barbara wondered if her voice sounded as unnatural to them as it seemed to her. 'The chalet has been closed up for five years.'

'Well I'm certainly glad you decided

to stop off here,' Jim said. 'Since your arrival everything seems to be going right for me.'

'Would you like me to look at your boat then?' Carter asked.

'Yes, please. And the sooner the better. When could you make it?'

'Any time that suits you. I only work part-time at the boat-yard these days.'

'I could drive you over tomorrow afternoon,' Barbara suggested.

'Right.' The old man nodded. 'That'll do me.'

'And I'll accompany you,' Jim said, glancing at Barbara. 'If you wouldn't mind,' he added. 'You'll need some extra help to get the boat out on the Broad. We'll come and pick you up at your place, Tom, about two-thirty.'

Tom Carter nodded and finished his drink. He departed, accompanied by Ruth. Jim took hold of Barbara's arm and led her to a table. He went back to the bar for a couple of drinks and then sat down opposite her.

'I'll come straight to the point,

Barbara,' Jim said earnestly. 'I'd like you to stay here as my assistant. That would put you in over Ruth, and it wouldn't take you long to settle her down. Should you accept the job I'd have no qualms about staying here. In fact I wouldn't dream of selling out, which would please Billy and Leanne, especially Leanne.'

'I'm working for you now,' Barbara said softly. 'So it doesn't really matter what position I hold. If you need an assistant more than a cook then I'll change jobs.'

'I'm interviewing two candidates tomorrow for the position you're filling at the moment — not that I expect to find anyone better than you, but you're capable of much more than running a kitchen and it would be criminal for me not to take advantage of that.'

'All right.' Barbara nodded. 'I'll work as your assistant.'

'Leanne will be so happy!' He raised his glass and toasted her. 'To your new job! It will be a pleasure to have you working with me. With your help I'll soon be right back on top. If I'm planning to stay then there's plenty of work to do.'

Barbara nodded as she glanced around. The bar was well filled with carefree holiday-makers. 'Count on me being here until the end of summer at least. Things quieten down around here then, I expect.'

'That's right, they do. But we maintain a steady stream of guests — enough to pay our way — through the winter.' He paused and drank from his glass, but his eyes were upon Barbara all the time, and she drew a deep breath.

'I'll review my situation again at the end of the summer,' Jim said thoughtfully.

'This is a good little hotel and it would be a pity to give it up. It was tough running the hotel without my wife beside me. The thrill had gone. But your arrival has given me another perspective.'

'Why don't you ask the company who wants to buy the hotel if the deadline can be extended till the end of the summer?' Barbara suggested casually.

'I might just do that, although I don't care much for their representative, Adrian Baybrooke. He seemed to have an eye for the main chance. A young chap handled the negotiations initially but I suspect Adrian edged him out. I must say, things have been going wrong ever since!'

'That's business these days,' Barbara responded. She was thinking frantically while Jim talked. As his assistant there was every chance she would bump into Adrian if he returned to discuss business. The problem seemed insoluble. Even buried in the kitchen there was still a chance Adrian might see her and she dreaded the outcome of that little scene.

'Something on your mind?' Jim queried, and she looked up to find him regarding her closely.

'I'm merely thinking about your problems,' she replied evasively.

'Spoken like a true assistant. You know, the job wouldn't be so bad. I'll be around most of the time, although I must confess that I do like the odd game of golf. But I'm sure there's nothing I could tell you about the business. And you'd get plenty of free time.'

'I like a game of golf myself,' Barbara responded. 'What's your handicap?'

'I've played off twelve, but lately I've taken to thrashing the ball.' He shook his head slowly. 'I've got to learn to settle down more. What's your handicap?'

'Fourteen.' She smiled.

He nodded slowly, his eyes half closed as he watched her. 'Yes,' he said slowly. 'I knew you'd be a perfectionist. Did you bring your golf clubs with you?'

'They're always in the boot of the car.' Barbara chuckled. 'Life is beginning to sound positively attractive. If you're serious about offering me a job as an assistant then I'm happy to accept.'

'Fine.' He reached across the table and took hold of her hand. 'Now we'll be going places! We'll make it official as soon as we find a full-time chef.'

She nodded. His eagerness and optimism were contagious and Barbara's spirit felt light as air. Jim's true nature was still something of a mystery to her but she sensed he was utterly trustworthy — a quality she valued highly. Now Barbara felt a growing need for Jim and a great desire to help him meet the challenge of building up his hotel business.

He had a lot going for him, she realised, struggling as he was against the aftermath of tragedy, trying to beat the grief that still clung to the recesses of his mind. Barbara herself knew what it was like to battle against the odds.

'You look thoughtful,' he remarked shortly.

'I'm just tired,' she countered with a

rueful smile. 'And I have to be up early in the morning.' She sighed regretfully. 'I've had a lovely evening, Jim. Thanks for taking me along. It was just what I needed.'

'I'll walk you up to your room.' He set down his glass and arose, pulling back her chair as she stood up. He held her arm as they walked to the door, and Barbara was only too aware of the rush of tenderness which surged through her breast. She felt suddenly vulnerable and wondered what kind of magic could have penetrated her armour of reserve, pushing all thoughts of Charles into the background of her mind.

When they reached the door of her room she fumbled in her bag for the key, but Jim took her hands in his and she looked up at him, swaying imperceptibly towards him, trapped in his aura of intangible magnetism.

'You're such a beautiful woman!' he said softly. 'I've never met anyone quite like you before. I don't know a thing about you, and I don't really care.'

'You're taking a great deal on trust,' she countered with a smile.

'Not really!' He shook his head. 'I've learned to trust my instincts.'

'What are they telling you?' Her tone was soft and her eyes were glowing.

'That you're one in a million and I'd be a prize fool if I let you slip away now that you've walked into my life.'

'Well, I'm not planning to slip away in the near future,' she said with a chuckle. 'I'm enjoying life too much to want to leave now.' She had to fight the unnerving impulse to thrust herself into his arms, for he was still holding her hands gently and their contact had heightened her senses unbearably. Her throat became constricted, and when she tried to speak to relieve the suddenly overpowering sense of passion which assailed her, she could think of nothing sensible to say.

'Life has definitely taken a turn for the better since your arrival,' he said softly. 'A couple of weeks ago I couldn't see any light at the end of the tunnel.

Now it's as if a blindfold has been removed from my eyes. I feel optimistic again. The hopelessness is fading and I'm beginning to look forward to life.'

'That's the spirit,' she encouraged. 'I know exactly how you're feeling because I've been through the same thing myself.'

'That's what I like about you.' He drew her slowly into his arms, pausing fleetingly to see if she would object, and when she did not stir he closed his arms about her, unmindful of the fact that they were standing in the corridor. 'I think you were sent straight from Heaven,' he said huskily.

Barbara caught her breath and willingly returned his embrace. He held her gently, as if afraid that she would break under pressure, and then kissed her. She closed her eyes and was swept upwards on a crest of desire.

His lips were gentle at first, caressing, and her fingers clutched at his shoulders. Then passion surged into him and his mouth became urgent and demanding, until Barbara felt as if she were being swept over a precipice in the grip of a tidal wave. They clung together ecstatically until they were forced to draw apart breathlessly.

Jim's eyes were shining as he searched her face for some visible reaction, and he must have read the pleasure that showed in her eyes and expression for he pulled her into his arms again and kissed her once more.

Barbara expected some kind of protest to form in her mind but desire gripped her instead and she responded feverishly, feeling like a young girl with her first love. The past five years had been devoid of sentiment and emotion. Adrian had made several clumsy attempts to seduce her but she had always strenuously resisted him. Jim was different, he might have been sent into her life for the sole purpose of ending her grief.

Jim eased back from her, and she could see that he was shaken by their embrace. He smiled.

'I think you'd better go now,' he said

gently. 'As much as I'd like you to stay with me we must keep our feet firmly planted on the ground. You've got to be up early in the morning, and I don't want you to overdo it. You're working like three people as it is.'

He paused and smiled again, his countenance softened by emotion. 'I'm very happy that you've turned up here the way you did. Good-night, Barbara. Sleep well. I'll see you in the morning.'

'Good-night, Jim!' she whispered, watched his retreating figure until he had disappeared down the stairs. Then she unlocked her door and slipped noiselessly into her room. Barbara's whole being tingled pleasurably and her mind was flooded with an overwhelming sense of elation.

7

When she slipped into bed, Barbara found it difficult to sleep despite the fact that she was very tired. Several times she made the effort to settle down only to stir and open her eyes to relive the precious moments of being held and kissed. She tried all the tricks she knew to induce sleep, but each time the burning imprint of Jim's lips against hers raised her from the depths of slumber and she stretched luxuriously, mulling over the situation.

How could two short weeks have wrought such a dramatic change in her life and Jim's? It was difficult now to recall exactly how she'd felt back in London, overworked and strained to the limit. She breathed deeply, her breast twisted by the most exquisite emotions. Her lips tingled and she sighed in pleasure, still feeling the touch of Jim's arms and mouth. Able to relax at last she drifted finally into blissful sleep.

All too soon the alarm clock was ringing stridently, and she opened her eyes and rolled over to stare at the faint sunlight peeping in at the open window. A smile played around the corner of her mouth as she recalled the way Jim had said good-night, and there was a sudden stirring of desire in her breast. She hurriedly got out of bed and began the routine of preparing for the kitchen, aware that shortly she would be assuming a different role.

Life was looking so much better, and when she remembered the pressures and frustrations of running Taylor Baybrooke, usually in opposition to Adrian, it all seemed like a ghastly nightmare. She was gripped by such a sense of revulsion that she knew she could never go back to it under any circumstances. She intended to leave her old life behind whatever the consequences and concentrate on matters close to her heart.

* * *

She was in the kitchen at six, and Billy was already there, smiling a welcome when he turned and saw her.

'You're up early, Billy,' she said.

'I was in here at five-thirty,' he responded. 'Did you see Tom Carter about servicing your boat?'

'Yes.' She nodded. 'We're going to take a look at it this afternoon, and if it's all right we can go out on Sunday, or any other day, come to that! Do you know how to handle a boat?'

'Oh yes! And Dad is a competent waterman.' He nodded confidently. 'We'll be able to handle it.' He paused and looked searchingly at her for a moment. 'Are you going to stay on here with us?' he asked at length.

'At least until the end of the summer.' She smiled when she saw his eyes light up. 'You seem to like the idea,' she ventured. 'I hope I can fit in around here.'

'You do that already without any

trouble.' He spoke with the candour of youth. 'And I can see a lot of changes coming, thanks to you.'

'All for the better, I hope.' Barbara smiled as she began making some tea for them as Billy prepared the toast. But all the time she was on edge for Jim's appearance. He had developed a habit of getting up very early and looking into the kitchen. This morning he did not arrive as usual and Barbara felt a keen sense of disappointment.

It had been surprisingly easy to cast off the yoke of five years grief and unrelenting work. There was no knowing what might happen now. But the past was irrelevant for she was happier at this moment than she had been at any time since Charles died.

'A penny for them!' Jim spoke cheerfully, and Barbara looked up to see him standing before her, a smile upon his face. 'You were miles away,' he commented. 'Not mulling over any guilty secrets, were you?'

'I didn't see you come in,' she

replied, fighting an urge to get closer to him. She wished that it was some other time, when they were both off duty. The intensity of her feelings was surprising.

'I've been catching up on some paperwork.' He shrugged. 'I think I'm going to delegate some of my responsibility in future. With a better trained staff there should be no problem. I believe in doing a full day's work myself, but I've been slaving away unnecessarily here, when I should have brought in extra help and given myself an easier time.'

'It's very easy to fall into that trap,' she responded with a wry smile. 'But it has its value. Hard work is the best way to overcome personal problems.'

'I agree, and I feel as if my troubles have all been whittled down to size.' He glanced around, saw that Billy was busy at the far end of the kitchen, and leaned forward, his tone dropping to a conspiratorial whisper. 'How are you feeling this morning?' he inquired. 'Did you sleep well?'

She could tell that he was fishing for a reaction to their embrace, and smiled as she nodded. 'I slept like a top! I suspect that last evening's outing agreed with me. I enjoyed it immensely. We'll certainly have to do it again.'

'I'm of the same opinion.' His eyes sparkled mischievously. 'Life has suddenly become worth living. Now about this afternoon. You finish in here at two. How quickly can you be ready to leave for your chalet?'

'I'll take a quick shower and change. That shouldn't take too long.'

'We'll go in my car then, and pick Tom up on the way. We'll wait until we find what state your boat is in before making any plans for Sunday, although we could easily take a drive on Sunday instead.'

'I'd like that!' She looked into his eyes and a thrill stabbed through her breast. She relived last night's embrace and yearned for the security of Jim's arms around her.

'Good.' He studied her eyes intently

and reached out to take her hand for a moment. A sigh escaped him and he shook his head. 'I wish the two of us were out on the golf course together right now,' he remarked. 'But business comes first, eh?' He glanced at his watch. 'Will you help Billy with the early morning teas? Pamela can't get in until seven-thirty.'

'Of course.' She smiled. But her expression sobered a little when he had departed. She had little idea of what was passing through his mind, and it was too early yet to jump to any conclusions. For herself, she seemed to be in a state of flux, and until she could think clearly she dared not try to make any kind of decision.

The morning passed quickly, and there didn't seem to be a spare moment. Leanne came in to see her before going off to school, still clutching her doll as if afraid to put it down for an instant. Then the cleaners came in for a cup of tea before taking up their particular duties. Mrs Moss arrived and started on the vegetables, her booming laugh echoing through the kitchen. Ruth appeared several times but always remained at a distance from Barbara, and finally Mrs Moss remarked upon it.

'Ruth's got it in for you, Barbara. Don't ever give her a chance to get at you. She's a nasty one, and no mistake.'

Barbara nodded, smiling, but there was a coldness inside her as she considered that there was great scope for Ruth to get at her, if only she knew!

When she went off duty it was a rush to get ready to leave at two-thirty, but she did it happily, and heaved a sigh of contentment when she finally sank into the front passenger seat of Jim's car. He joined her, and Barbara experienced a momentary pang of disquiet when she saw Ruth peering at them from a window. But she soon forgot her as they left the hotel, chatting animatedly. Barbara was happy to be in Jim's company, and she could see that he was at ease with her.

They picked up Tom Carter and

drove to Horning. Barbara gave directions until they reached the chalet, and Jim whistled appreciatively when he studied the place. But she noticed that there was a slight frown upon his forehead as they alighted from the car.

'The boathouse is over there.' She led the way, searching in her handbag for the keys, and when she opened the door and Jim saw Lady Barbara he paused in surprise and shook his head in wonder.

'That is a boat and a half!' he remarked, glancing at her. 'And you say it hasn't been out in five years?'

'I haven't been here in all that time,' she responded. 'My son has been here several times, I seem to remember, but I don't know if he ever used the boat. I have the chalet maintained, and perhaps he arranged for someone to keep an eye on the boat.'

'I would hope so!' Jim nodded. 'I would if it were mine.'

'I'll soon tell you if it's watertight,' Tom said, moving forward. 'Then we'll get her out of the boathouse and see if we can start the engine. Will you get the front doors open, Jim? We can hoist the sail if the motor won't fire.'

'I'll leave you to it,' Barbara decided. 'I'll go into the chalet and make myself useful. There must be some tidying up to be done. Some of Charles's things should be put out.'

'Go ahead,' Jim replied. 'We'll give you a call if we need you.'

Barbara took the keys and went across to the chalet. She unlocked the door before pausing to glance back at the boathouse. Jim was opening the doors at the water's edge. Tom Carter had already disappeared inside the boat itself.

For a moment Barbara's mind browsed in the past, looking for the solace she had always sought from memory. But, surprisingly, she did not need any props for her emotions. She glanced around keenly, and decided to check there was no evidence of her real identity lying round. At the moment she was plain Mrs Lennard. If Jim saw anything which linked her to Taylor Baybrooke then she would be in dire trouble.

At first it was painful to open drawers and look into cupboads and find things that had belonged to Charles, or reminded her of their past life together. But there was a new-found strength in her mind and she threw herself into the task with determination. Time passed unnoticed, until Jim coughed discreetly and she looked up from delving into a cupboard to see him standing in the doorway of her bedroom.

'Hello, you look busy,' he remarked.

'I am!' She nodded. 'Doing a job that should have been done years ago. How are you getting on with the boat?'

'I suspect that your son has been using it pretty frequently. The hull is watertight, and there's a sticker on the engine indicating that it was serviced three months ago.'

'Good!' She nodded. 'So it's ship-shape?'

'Of course. Would you like a short

trip? Tom thinks we should give it a run, and he's the expert. If there is anything wrong he can soon put it right.'

'All right.' She got to her feet and surveyed the untidiness around her. 'I can always finish this job later.'

They left the chalet and she locked the door. As they walked to the water's edge, Barbara saw Lady Barbara moored to the bank, dazzling white in the sunlight. Tom stood at the wheel in the cabin and waved a hand as Barbara approached.

Jim helped her aboard, and Barbara experienced a pang of nostalgia as she stepped into the cabin. The engine was throbbing rhythmically, just as it had when Charles was at the helm, but the memory was not so hurtful now and she was thankful as she sat down in her customary place and relaxed. Jim sat beside her while Tom exhibited his skill in handling the craft.

She studied Jim's profile while his gaze was averted, and liked what she saw. The future was hers if she had the courage to reach out and take it. Barbara found it difficult to accept the strength of her feelings for Jim especially when she knew nothing of his emotions. She blinked, for Jim had turned his head and was now contemplating her, and she was still gazing unashamedly at him, her mind busy. He smiled at her sudden discomfiture.

'You seemed a long way off just then,' he remarked. 'Was it time or distance?'

'Probably a little of both,' she admitted quietly. 'You can guess when I was last on this boat. There are ghosts aboard with us, but they are finding their rightful places at last.'

'I know what you mean.' He nodded soberly. 'I'm coming to terms with my wife's death at last but it has taken me a very long time. He reached out and took hold of her hand. 'I never thought I'd be able to look at another woman,' he went on softly. 'But you're special, Barbara, and there's no-one else to touch you in my life.'

Barbara settled back, content to let Jim take command of the situation, and her eyes softened as she regarded him.

'I feel the same,' she admitted. Emotion touched her and she swallowed inaudibly. 'I don't know what made me stop off at your hotel when I arrived. I could have come straight on to the chalet. But I'm thankful now for that sudden impulse.'

'Are you?' His eyes gleamed and his grip upon her hand tightened convulsively. 'I sensed that all was not well with you as soon as I saw you. Call it intuition if you like, but you seemed — different at first glance. Now, of course, I know you're in a class by yourself.'

Barbara looked out over the bows. A sailing yacht with a tall mast and pale blue sails was tacking in front of them, and Tom put the wheel over a couple of points to avoid it. He called some good-natured advice to the sailor, who waved a nonchalant hand. Barbara inhaled deeply. The vividness of the sunny day was almost too bright for her eyes, and pleasure was sharp in her mind. Memories of London and her big office in the hotel crept unbidden into her mind but she shrank from the thought and turned back to Jim, squeezing his hand as a thrill darted through her.

'You don't have any problems with this craft,' Tom called from the wheel. 'Shall we run into Horning and fill up with fuel? She'll need topping up if you're going out at the week-end.'

'Do that, Tom,' Jim said without hesitation, smiling at Barbara. 'We're certainly going out on Sunday, come rain or shine.'

It was a relief for someone else to take the initiative. For the past five years Barbara had had to make all the decisions. Now she wanted to relax and let others take the responsibility. Jim seemed equal to the task, and probably needed the opportunity to show that he could still do it.

She smiled as she gazed ahead,

watching the ever changing surface patterns of the Broads. Fleecy white clouds cast their shadows upon the bright water, and she realised she'd been living her life in the shadows since Charles died, but now the bad memories were fading and she could look forward to happiness.

* * *

When they finally returned to the boathouse, Tom Carter was extravagant in his praise of Lady Barbara and Jim was itching to take over and put the craft through its paces. But it was moored under cover, and Barbara went into the chalet to check that everywhere was tidy before they returned to the hotel. They dropped Tom at his home and, when they were alone and driving back to the hotel, Jim glanced at her as he sighed rather heavily.

'Life is strange, isn't it?' he mused. 'I spent most of my young life working towards an ideal, the realisation of a dream, and, just when it seemed that I had it in my grasp, my wife died and nothing seemed to matter any more. But time passed, and just when I'd lost all hope of happiness, you came into my life. I find myself at a crossroads now, and I have a feeling that you are in the same predicament. It's hard to understand, but it's a relief after so many empty years.'

Barbara nodded. 'I'm thankful I've survived this far,' she said thoughtfully. 'But the trick is to continue making progress.' She glanced at his profile, relieved that his attention was upon the road for it gave her a chance to observe him closely and she experienced a tiny fluttering of her pulses at his magnetic attraction.

'I didn't get the chance to tell you earlier,' he said suddenly. 'But I engaged a new chef this morning. He'll be coming to take over the kitchen on Sunday. Would you assume the duties of Assistant Manager on Monday?'

'With pleasure!' She spoke without

hesitation. 'But we ought to chat about policy and administration. I don't think the hotel is living up to its full potential.'

'You're right, and you're very perceptive if you've realised that in the short time you've been here. This present state of affairs is entirely my own fault, but now I shall be doing everything possible to push us back on top. I'll give you a free hand to run the place. I am getting back to my old self, but I think I need you to do the vital work of reorganisation.'

'That sounds fine.' She nodded as he brought the car to a halt in front of the hotel, and Leanne appeared as if from nowhere, carrying her doll, and came running to greet them. 'I like a challenge,' she said, waving to Leanne. 'It will be quite a refreshing exercise to bring this place back from the dead.'

Jim chuckled, but shook his head ruefully when she looked at him. 'You're being brutal,' he remarked. 'But I deserve it for letting the business slide to such a degree.'

'I'm only stating the truth.' Barbara smiled. 'I understand only too well what happened but it's a good sign that you want to change. I'll do whatever I can to help.'

'You've already done more than anyone could hope for,' he responded, opening his door. 'And not only for me personally. I can see a big difference in Leanne.' He chuckled as Leanne reached Barbara's door. 'Just look at her face! She's so pleased to see you. And note that it's you she's run to, not me, and I'm her father!'

'She's been missing a caring woman around her,' Barbara said.

'Not just any woman.' Jim smiled. 'Ruth has tried for a long time to make Leanne like her, but she couldn't succeed in a hundred years. Yet when you came along, Leanne took to you almost at once.'

'Hello, Barbie,' Leanne called, pulling open the car door. 'I've been looking everywhere for you.'

'We've been checking my boat,' Barbara said, reaching out and squeezing Leanne's hand. 'It'll be all right for Sunday, if we can all get off duty.' She got out of the car and took hold of Leanne's hand, and they stood waiting for Jim to join them. Then they walked into the hotel together, and Barbara sighed with contentment. Right now this was all she needed!

8

Jim excused himself and went into his office to do some paperwork. Barbara offered to keep Leanne company but as they went up to Barbara's room, Billy appeared from his cubby-hole, a frown on his face. He followed Barbara up the stairs until they were out of sight of the lobby, where Ruth was sitting behind the desk, and then called to Barbara, who turned with a smile upon her face.

'How'd you find the boat?' Billy asked.

'All right. We'll be going out on Sunday.' Barbara noted Billy's seriousness, and paused. 'Is something wrong, Billy?'

'I'm not sure, but I've a bad feeling about this.' He glanced down the stairs before going on. 'Just after you left with Dad earlier I went up to check the bathroom on your floor, and I saw Ruth in the corridor directly outside your room with a pass key in her hand. I think she had just come out of your room and was locking the door. If I'd been a few minutes earlier I would have caught her in the act.'

Barbara's expression was grim. Leanne was staring up at her, obviously wondering what to make of it all, and Billy was shaking his head slowly.

'I do know that Ruth has been trying to unearth information about you,' Billy went on. 'There isn't a day goes by that she doesn't make some comment about you — usually unflattering.'

'I see.' Barbara smiled. 'Well, thanks for telling me, Billy. But Ruth can go into my room any time she likes. I have nothing to hide and there's nothing in my room that could interest her. We'll say nothing to her about this, and you needn't even mention it to your father. He'd probably be very angry and then there would be trouble. Let's forget about it, shall we?'

Billy nodded. 'I intend to keep an eye

on her after this,' he vowed.

Barbara tightened her clasp upon Leanne's hand. 'You can talk to me while I wash my hair.'

Leanne accompanied her eagerly, and Barbara gave the girl some old make-up to play with. After washing and drying her hair, Barbara discovered that Leanne had been experimenting, with bizarre results.

'Let me show you how it's done,' she said gently, removing the smear of lipstick from Leanne's face with a tissue.

Leanne was a willing pupil and time passed unnoticed. All too soon there was a knock at the door. Barbara opened it to find Jim outside.

'Is Leanne with you?' he asked. 'It's time she went to bed.'

'Come in.' Barbara held the door wide and he entered. When he saw Leanne he stopped and held up his hands.

'Please excuse me,' he said very seriously. 'I didn't know you had company, Barbara. Who is this very beautiful lady?'

'I'm not a lady, I'm Leanne wearing make-up! Barbara showed me how to put it on.' Leanne chuckled merrily.

'Leanne?' Jim shook his head in surprise. 'Not the Leanne whose father owns the hotel? I don't believe it!' He advanced upon her, leaning forward to peer more intently at her, and Leanne subsided into giggles.

'You do look like her,' he admitted, glancing at Barbara, who nodded silently. 'But there is something wrong with your mouth. Did you cut yourself shaving this morning, Leanne?'

'It's lipstick!' Leanne shouted at him, greatly amused. 'Barbie wears it and she looks good in it.'

'And so do you, my pet!' Jim swept her up into his arms and kissed her, taking care not to smudge her lipstick. 'Now it's time for bed, so say good-night to Barbie and let's get you settled.'

'Barbie can take me to bed,' Leanne said instantly, turning an appealing gaze towards Barbara, who didn't want to intrude since this was probably one of the few occasions when father and daughter could spend time together in a busy day.

Jim shrugged. 'So I've been discarded in favour of another,' he said melodramatically.

'You can come as well, Daddy! I'd like that!'

'Why don't I indeed?' He nodded. 'If Barbie will remove your lipstick now!' He waited until Barbara had complied, and then went to the door with Leanne in his arms. 'Are you coming, Barbie?' he demanded. 'Or have you had too much of this child for one day?'

'I'm coming,' Barbara responded as Leanne gazed imploringly at her. 'And she's been very good company today, as always. If we do decide to go out for the day on Sunday then I think she can be allowed to go with us.'

'Are we going out on Sunday?' Leanne demanded as they went along to her room.

'If you're a good girl.' Jim paused, and then added, 'But I'm forgetting that you're always a good girl, Leanne, and I'm very grateful for that.'

Barbara tried to stay in the background to give Jim time alone with his daughter, but Leanne would have none of it and kept drawing Barbara into their conversation. But finally the girl was settled down and Barbara and Jim left the room. He heaved a sigh as he closed the door.

'That should be the last we hear from her this evening. She's grown very attached to you.' He sighed. 'I've got some more paperwork to take care of right now. Shall I see you in the bar later?'

'If you like.'

'I would like!' He looked at her closely. 'I'll look into the bar about nine-fifteen.'

'I'll be there,' she promised. 'In the meantime I think I'll go for a short drive.'

* * *

They parted in the lobby and Barbara set off in her car to find a public telephone. Calling Derek, she was pleased when his voice sounded at the other end of the line, and when she spoke he replied cheerfully.

'Mother! It's good to hear your voice! Are you enjoying yourself?'

'Very much. I've never felt better. Leaving London was the best thing that ever happened to me.'

'I just wish you'd tell me where you are. I can't help worrying about you. Your voice at the end of a telephone doesn't really tell me anything.'

'That's how I like it at the moment. Now listen to me, Derek. I've met someone I want to help. He's very interested in the hotel business. I want you to check around and see if we can fit him in somewhere with us.'

'Who have you found, Mother?' Alarm filled Derek's voice. 'You can't be too careful these days! I know I shouldn't have to tell you that, but you were acting so strangely before you ran off!'

'Ran off!' Barbara chuckled. 'I didn't run off. I merely became sick to death of the situation that had arisen at Head Office! But I'll tell you this much! There'll be some changes when I do come back.'

'That's what I like to hear!' He chuckled. 'So tell me about this man you've met who wants to be a hotelier.'

'Did I say he was a man?' she said sharply.

'It is a male, you said!'

'Yes, and don't take that tone with me, Derek! Billy is about sixteen years old and he hasn't had the opportunities you were blessed with. I bent a few rules to put you in where you are at present, and I've carried you a great deal because you are my son.'

'All right, Mother! Don't be so touchy. We can easily absorb a youngster. What do you have in mind for him?'

'I want him to learn the business from bottom to top, starting with a management and catering course. I'll leave you to work out some details before I call again.'

'What's his name, Mother?' Derek sounded distant, but she ignored the fact.

'That doesn't matter at the moment. Now tell me what Adrian has been up to.'

'There's bad news about the Farrell hotel in Norfolk, I'm afraid!' Derek chuckled despite the apparent setback. 'All Adrian has managed to do is scare Farrell off. He now wants to extend the time limit we arranged. He's going to sit tight until the end of the summer season.'

Barbara smiled. 'Is that so? I'd better ring Adrian and get a report from him. In future perhaps he'll be more careful about interfering.'

'If you hand the negotiations back to me I'll see if I can repair the damage Adrian has done.' There was an eager note in Derek's voice.

'Not for the moment. Just do as I ask

and I'll be satisfied. Have you any problems that you can't cope with?'

'None. It's very quiet with you out of the office.'

'Fine. Let's hope it stays that way. I'll call you again. Don't forget to work out a plan of campaign for young Billy. 'Bye for now.'

''Bye, Mother.'

Barbara rang off before Derek could say anything more. She thought for a moment, then called Adrian. The phone rang for some moments and she began to feel impatient, thinking that he was out, but at length the receiver at the other end was lifted and a woman's voice spoke.

'Hello. This is Mr Adrian Baybrooke's residence.'

Barbara bit her lip against a retort and paused for a moment to recollect her thoughts.

'Is Adrian at home?' she demanded.

'He is. Who shall I say is calling?'

'Just get him to the phone, please.'

'One moment. He's in the shower.'

Barbara hung on, and shortly Adrian's voice sounded in her ear. He was breathless.

'Hello, Adrian, sorry to cut into your off-duty time, but I wasn't able to call during office hours.'

'Barbara! That's all right. I don't mind when you call me. I was wondering about you, as a matter of fact.'

'I'm fine. Just tell me about the Farrell hotel.'

'Tell you what about it?' There was a blustering note in his voice.

'What's the current situation? I left you handling the deal and I want a progress report. I'm very interested in this piece of business, as you know.'

'I'm afraid that Farrell is cooling off somewhat. He's asking to extend our deadline. We'll have to wait until the end of the season now.'

'So you've made a mess of it!' Barbara sounded stern. 'I handed the job to Derek and you saw fit to take it away from him when he was doing so well. This is not good enough, Adrian.'

'I'm planning to go to Norfolk this week-end to put some pressure on Farrell. I think I know what's happening behind the scenes, but I need to make an on-the-spot check.'

'What could be happening behind the scenes?' Barbara was instantly alert.

'I have a contact at Farrell's hotel. The receptionist, Ruth Carter! She rings me frequently, and the last time I spoke to her she said there's a woman staying at the hotel who seems to be manipulating Farrell. Perhaps he's falling in love!

'Anyway, this woman has given him fresh hope and they're working together as a team. So I thought I'd go there and try different tactics.'

'No. Don't do that!' Barbara tried not to sound unduly alarmed.

'Why not? We still want the hotel, don't we?'

'It's giving us more trouble than it's worth, thanks to you. I suggest you forget about Farrell and his hotel for the moment. Leave the matter until I return. If Farrell wants an extension, give in on that point. Do I make myself clear?'

'Yes. But I'd like to give it one more try.'

'You haven't listened to a word I've said Adrian! No wonder I almost worked myself into a nervous breakdown! So let's try it once more, shall we, and see if you can grasp the situation?'

'All right. No need to take that tone! I'll hand the whole thing back to Derek.'

'Good. That's very good. Give Derek my instructions. I'm sorry I've interrupted your evening. Goodbye now. You'll be hearing from me again in due course.'

'Barbara! Don't hang up yet.' He suddenly sounded urgent.

'You have a companion with you now,' she replied. 'Don't be greedy, Adrian. Goodbye.' She replaced the receiver, and there was a wry smile upon her lips as she left the telephone box.

But when she was driving back to the hotel her expression hardened. So Ruth was in almost daily contact with Adrian, passing on details of Jim's business; selling him out, in effect. But what could she do about that? Then she thought of her own position. Sooner or later Jim would have to know the truth. Shouldn't she make some effort now to reveal her true identity. If he should stumble across the fact by accident, would he think she'd had something to hide?

It was quite a problem, she thought, as she parked the car in front of the hotel, and she was reluctant to shatter the tentative bonds she'd forged with Jim and his family. Finally, she decided to sleep on it. Perhaps inspiration would strike in the morning.

Jim was in the bar, and her heartbeats quickened when she saw him. He came to meet her, smiling, his eyes filled with eagerness. Barbara glanced around for a glimpse of the ever-present Ruth, but for once the receptionist was absent.

'Hello.' Jim took her hand briefly. 'Glad you've decided to come back.' He paused. 'Are you in touch with your family? They might be worrying about you.'

'It's all right.' She smiled. 'I've spoken to my son. I still maintain that I haven't run away from anything, if that is what you mean.'

'Come and have a drink. We can talk about what to do on Sunday. I can have the day off, and there's someone to cover the kitchen in your absence. I've been pulling Billy's leg about it, saying that I can't spare him, but of course he can come along.'

He paused, holding her elbow, and looked into her eyes. His fingers dug into her arm for a moment, and then he smiled and seated her at a table in an alcove.

Barbara glanced around while she waited for his return, and spotted Ruth seated in the opposite corner with two youngish men. Yet again, Barbara wondered what the girl was after. If she wanted Jim for herself then surely she wouldn't betray him to Adrian. Unless she wanted Jim to sell out and move! That must be it. Barbara frowned as she watched Ruth. She'd never met anyone so selfish or eroded by malice. Barbara hoped that Jim could take care of himself.

Jim came back to the table, and Barbara wondered if she should try to reveal a little of her true background. She tried to imagine what he would say if he knew who she really was! She sipped her drink, watching his profile as he gazed around the bar, and he turned his attention to her after studying the guests.

'You look very chic this evening,' he commented.

'Thank you.' She smiled.

'I mean that. I'm not given to empty flattery.' He set down his glass and studied her, really looking at her.

Barbara felt her muscles tense. 'You are full of surprises. I've had a good look at your hands, and I'd be surprised if you have done any kitchen work in the last fifteen years. Then there's your holiday chalet and boat! My God! I'm in the hotel business and I can't afford anything like that.'

'The trappings of success,' she countered.

'Your clothes are the best. I expect you live in a mansion somewhere down in the south of England, and have a dozen servants. You came here in a Ford Escort, but I suspect you're more at home in a Mercedes sports car at least.'

'Would you like an offical rundown on me?' she asked with a smile.

'No.' He shook his head. 'I've told you that it doesn't matter. You'll tell me all about yourself when you are good and ready.'

She nodded, aware that he had given her an opening to broach the subject of her past life. But she didn't know how to begin. She fancied that if he learned the truth the shock might turn him against her, and she couldn't afford to run that risk. He waited patiently, giving her time to think, but she closed her lips firmly. In her experience indecision meant wait and get it right.

'I've put out some feelers for Billy.' She changed the subject.

'Thank you. He's certainly keen to get away from home and spread his wings.' Jim smiled, but his eyes betrayed the fact that he was concerned about his son. 'Where would you have him go if you can help him?'

'London, of course. It's all happening there these days.'

'He would certainly have a marvellous opportunity if you could help him. Do you run a hotel, Barbara?'

'Not as such.' She paused, although she realised she couldn't leave it at that. 'Look, I'm not really reluctant to tell you about myself. It's just that I came here incognito, so to speak, and for the time being I'd like it to remain that way.'

'That's all right! I shan't force the issue. But it's difficult to hold a normal conversation without your background cropping up from time to time.'

'I feel I ought to tell you something,' she hedged.

'You don't have to.' He sipped his drink.

'I was working in London,' she said cautiously. 'I booked in here under my maiden name.'

'That's a natural thing to do if you wanted to keep your presence here a secret.' He eyed her for a moment. 'Have you told anyone yet where you are?'

'No. I've used the telephone so they know I'm all right.'

'Why did you go to such lengths?' There was genuine concern in his eyes, and he reached across the table and covered her fingers.

'I was utterly sick of the life I'd been leading, and it seemed the right thing to do at the time.'

'So you're living a lie!'

'At the moment, yes. I don't like it, but that's the way it is.'

Barbara wanted desperately to confide in Jim but couldn't find the words. Jim finished his drink, started to rise, and the opportunity passed.

'I have to chat to some of the guests in the hotel,' he said. 'Will you wait for me?'

'Certainly!' She nodded.

He smiled and departed, and Barbara sat back in her seat and heaved a sigh. If only she'd had the courage to tell him the truth! Barbara regretted the deception but how could she have known that Jim Farrell would mean so much to her?

While she was grappling with the situation and trying to reach a decision, Ruth appeared before her, slipping into the seat that Jim had vacated.

'It's about time someone set you straight,' she said without preamble. 'You're making a complete fool of yourself. But that's only natural, I suppose, seeing that you're a complete stranger.'

'I don't understand.' Barbara frowned.

'You will now. I've seen the way you've been looking at Jim. And he's making it seem that you're the only woman in the world! But don't be fooled by his manner. You're not the first woman he's been attracted to since his wife died and I don't suppose you'll be the last.

'There was a time when I hoped he'd look in my direction, but that's not his style. He prefers a variety of women, and he's in the right job to gratify his desires.'

'Thank you for the warning.' Barbara smiled, although it seemed that a cold hand clutched at her heart. 'But there's no need to concern yourself about my welfare. I'm quite able to take care of myself.'

'Are you planning to stay on here? I thought you were on holiday!'

'I don't know what my long-term plans are.' Barbara shook her head. 'I'll let you know when I reach a decision.'

Ruth smiled oversweetly and got to her feet. 'You think I'm trying to feather my own nest, don't you? Well, don't say you haven't been warned.'

Barbara moistened her lips as Ruth departed, and a sigh escaped her as she considered how best to handle the muddle she'd created for herself. She wished with all her heart that she hadn't come to the hotel under false pretences, and was uncomfortably aware that any information Ruth discovered about her would be presented to Jim in the worst possible light.

Suddenly the whole affair had become urgent, and she realised that she ought to have considered the consequences of arriving at the hotel unannounced. What had started off as an innocent deception was now a rather serious problem because she had become involved with the Farrell family.

Jim returned some minutes later, a

tender smile appearing on his face, and Barbara felt elated at the sight of him. An intangible thrill spread through her, and she was aware that if she had to face the future without seeing him again she would be extremely unhappy. She could only hope for a peaceful outcome to her dilemma.

9

Barbara invited Jim into her room when he escorted her from the bar later, determined to broach the subject of her true identity. He unlocked the door for her and stepped aside. She brushed his shoulder in passing and he placed a hand upon her upper arm. Barbara turned to him, barely giving him room to close the door. He took her tenderly into his arms, kissing her with fervour. She closed her eyes and let pleasure sweep through her body.

It was only now that she realised just how much she had missed the company of a man since Charles died. She had lived in the past since his demise, but life was for the living. She knew that now, and wanted to grasp the opportunity with both hands.

'I'm revising a lot of the principles by which I live,' Jim said softly in her ear, his breath warm against her cheek. 'I built a shrine to my wife in my heart and never looked at another woman after she died.

'Now you've come along, and in an unbelievably short time I've willingly torn down all my defences and opened up my feelings. I've regained my spirit and the will to forget the past. It's no good for a man to be on his own, Barbara.'

'Haven't you been out with a woman since your wife died?' Barbara asked in such a way that Jim drew back from her and peered intently into her face.

'I haven't,' he said firmly. 'What makes you ask?'

Barbara shook her head. 'It doesn't matter. I was only asking, and really, it's none of my business.'

'Someone's been talking to you! Was it Ruth? Come, Barbie, tell me! I don't want any misunderstandings. One thing I cannot stand is deceit. I could overlook a multitude of sins, but a liar slams the door in my face.'

'Ruth did warn me off earlier, but I think we both know what she is like.' Barbara turned away and went to put her handbag on the dressing table. She noticed that her document case was sticking out of the top right hand drawer, and frowned as she picked it up and opened it. Her driving licence lay inside, with her passport, but they were not in their individual compartments.

Jim strode across the room and grasped her arm. 'Barbara, what did Ruth have to say?' he demanded.

'It doesn't matter, Jim. Forget it. I know what she's up to so no harm has been done.'

He looked at her, his eyes filled with a calculating light. Then he sighed heavily. 'She's been slandering me, hasn't she? Did she tell you that I'd been going out with other women?' Anger showed in his eyes. 'By Heaven! I've put up with a lot from her, but if she is trying to interfere with my personal life then she's overstepped the mark.'

'There's been no harm done,' Barbara insisted. 'I paid no attention to her. In any case, I rely on my judgement of a person's character.'

'Nevertheless, I'm going to have a word with her about this. I've turned a blind eye until now because she was a close friend of my wife. But the old Jim Farrell is back now, and I'm going to act differently from now on.' He paused, looked intently into her face, and then sighed and drew her into his arms.

Barbara closed her eyes as he kissed her, and responded instinctively. Her heart pounded as she slid her arms around his shoulders, clasping him with increasing fervour. It occurred to her that this was what was wrong with her life. She needed a man to fill the great void left by Charles' death — not just any man but someone like Jim, who could love her for herself alone.

'Good-night, Barbara,' he said quietly as he released her. 'I've still got a number of things to do before I can call it a day. You know how it is. For months I've been letting things slide, doing just enough to get through. But, as I say, all that has changed now. I'll see you in the morning.'

'Good-night, Jim.' A tremor tingled through her breast as she let him go. She longed to call him back, but reluctantly remained silent as he smiled and departed. Her mind was full of conflicting emotions, but there was no denying the fact that she was well and truly in love with Jim Farrell!

She fell asleep thinking about him, and just before she lapsed into unconsciousness she had decided that she had no alternative but to tell Jim all about herself, as soon as possible. With that decision made, she slept deeply, and did not stir until the alarm clock disturbed her slumber the next morning.

Going down to the kitchen at six, Barbara found Billy already there, preparing the early morning teas. He turned to her with a ready smile.

'Hello, Barbara. I'm glad about

Sunday. That boat of yours should be given a good run if she's been tied up in the boathouse for any length of time.'

'I'm quite looking forward to it myself,' Barbara responded. 'And you'll be pleased to hear that I've made some inquiries about you going to a hotel in London, Billy.'

'Have you really?' His eyes sparkled with excitement. 'Do you think I'll get a chance?'

'You can take it from me.' She nodded. 'You have every chance in the world.'

'That's great! Thank you, Barbara.' He smiled and returned to his work. Then he looked up. 'Oh, I almost forgot. There was a note from Dad under my door this morning when I awoke. He had to go on business last night. He said he'd be back as soon as possible, but not to worry if he wasn't around early this morning.

'Something must have come up unexpectedly.' Billy shrugged. 'There is a big change in Dad these days. I think it's because you're here, Barbara.'

Leanne appeared just before she had to leave for school.

'I can't find Dad anywhere this morning.' Leanne clutched her doll.

'Is there something worrying you, Leanne?' Barbara demanded. 'Does someone usually take you to school or are you allowed to go alone?'

'I often go alone. I'm not worried about anything, Barbie. I was only looking at you.'

Barbara smiled. 'You must know what my face looks like by now. Is there anything you want before you go to school?'

'No, thank you.' Leanne held up her face for a kiss and Barbara obliged. 'I'll see you when I come home. I put flowers on my mother's grave every week on this afternoon. If you're not busy later will you go with me?'

'Of course! I'll be here when you come home.' Barbara watched the girl to the kitchen door, which opened to admit Jim as Leanne reached it.

'Daddy!' Leanne cried. 'I've been waiting to see if you'd come home. I've got to go to school now.'

'Very well. You'd better run along, Sugar! I'm pretty busy right now.'

'All right. But when I come out of school Barbie is going with me to the cemetery.'

'I doubt if she'll still be here then, Leanne!' Jim's face was haggard, and his eyes glittered as he looked at Barbara. 'Mrs Taylor will probably be going back to London after we've had a chat.'

'Who's Mrs Taylor? She's got nothing to do with us!' Leanne cried.

'You're right!' Jim's voice was rough with suppressed emotion.

'What on earth are you talking about?' Barbara demanded. 'What's happened, Jim?'

He shrugged wearily and shook his head, while Leanne clutched at his hand and began to cry. Jim's shoulders slumped dejectedly. 'Ruth cornered me last night after I left your room. She'd discovered your real identity. At first I refused to believe it, but she gave me Adrian's personal phone number and I called him. He told me how you'd thought up the idea of coming here incognito to soften me up.'

He paused, shaking his head, and then chuckled hollowly. 'You made a good job of that, didn't you? I kept saying that he had the wrong woman, so I drove to London to see him and he showed me a photograph of you. Quite a celebrity in the upper circles, aren't you?'

He chuckled, a harsh, bitter sound that was filled with disillusionment. 'So you fooled me! But you won't get your hands on this hotel, Mrs Taylor! We've had quite enough!'

Barbara could not think coherently and there was a numb sensation in her breast. Leanne was crying, and the sound of it tore across Barbara's nerves. The girl suddenly turned and ran from the kitchen. Billy dropped a saucepan with a resounding crash, and Jim shook his head as he hurried after his daughter. Barbara could hear him calling Leanne's name in the lobby. She looked at Billy, who was staring at her, his face filled with shock and pain. Then her thoughts started working again and a torrent of emotion swept through her.

Hastily removing her apron, she approached Billy, but he turned and left the kitchen by the back entrance. Barbara stared at the swinging door for a moment, tears welling up in her eyes. Sighing bitterly she turned and hurried to her room. In a matter of minutes she had packed, but there was misery in her heart as she struggled down the stairs with her cases.

So Ruth had finally won! Barbara fought the rising tide of her emotions. As she got into the Escort she glanced at the hotel with tears shimmering in her eyes. Blinking rapidly, she saw Leanne suddenly peering from a ground floor window and sobbing uncontrollably, her doll clasped to her chest. The sight almost tore Barbara's heart in two. Then Jim appeared, pulling the girl away. Barbara choked on a sob and drove out of the car park.

She was stiff and shocked, filled with desolation as she drove heedlessly on, not stopping the car until she reached London and parked in front of her home . . .

* * *

After a shower and a change of clothing, Barbara felt more human, although there was a cold chill in her breast. She checked the time and saw that she could get to her office before business ended for the day, so she took her Daimler. There was a tearing hurt in her thoughts and she could feel unhappiness sawing relentlessly at her self-esteem.

Her desk was occupied by Derek, who was leafing through a newspaper. He looked up at her entrance and then sprang to his feet, astounded by her appearance.

'Mother! You're back!' he gasped.

'Obviously! Call Adrian and tell him to come here. Move out of my seat.'

'Yes, Mother!' Derek moved hurriedly, frowning as he picked up the telephone. 'I've got the details you want for young Billy. They are on the desk.'

'I doubt if they'll be needed now.' Barbara pressed trembling fingers to her throbbing temples. 'Get Adrian in here and don't tell him that I'm back.'

A few moments later the door opened and Adrian entered the office. He paused on the threshold to stare for a moment at Barbara then shrugged and closed the door before coming to the desk. He sat down beside Derek, and Barbara watched him intently until he was settled. The atmosphere seemed to close in about them.

'So you came back!' Adrian smiled thinly.

'Why did you lie to Jim Farrell about me?' she demanded harshly.

He sighed heavily. 'It was for the good of the company. When Ruth rang to say she had searched your room and found out who you really were, I assumed that you had gone to Farrell's hotel to check out the situation for yourself, knowing what a stickler you are. But Ruth said you were getting emotionally involved with Farrell, and I didn't see that as an asset.'

'It certainly wouldn't further your ambitions. I can see that.' Barbara suppressed a sigh. 'So you lied when Jim arrived in London. You told him I had gone to Norfolk to spy on him.'

'That's right, and it must have been quite effective or you wouldn't be here now. I don't know what you really had in mind, but it's a good thing we've stopped it. And you'll thank me when you've come to your senses.

'Get out of here, Adrian, and try to stay out of my way as much as possible in future.'

Adrian shook his head and sighed heavily before turning to the door.

Barbara called to him.

'Give the Farrell file to Derek, please,' she said crisply. 'As from this moment you have no further responsibility for it.' She glanced at her son. 'Go with him, Derek, and get that file.'

Derek went after Adrian, and Barbara leaned back in her seat, shaking with conflicting emotions. It was Thursday, she told herself, and only this morning she had been looking forward to Sunday. Now there was a black void in her heart and the future stretched ahead like a desert, bleak and inhospitable. Then impatience stirred her and she felt a touch of her old spirit.

Why shouldn't she return to Norfolk, confront Jim and tell him the truth? If he had any real feelings for her he would surely listen! Then she pictured his face as she had last seen it and despair flooded her. His mind had been poisoned by lies, and he would never believe her now.

Derek returned with the Farrell file and laid it upon the desk without a word. Barbara stared at it, reading Jim's name on the cover, and she had to clench her teeth against the urge to cry.

'Do you want to talk about it, Mother?' Derek asked softly, and she stared at him for a moment, dry-eyed but hurting. 'I gather you've been in Norfolk. When you telephoned last you sounded so happy and carefree.'

'I'd rather not talk about it,' she said with a catch in her voice.

'Is Billy, Jim Farrell's son?'

'Yes. He's Billy Farrell.'

'And do you want me to offer him a position with us?'

'Yes. That's the least I can do.' She nodded, picturing Billy's face. 'Make an attractive offer, Derek.'

'Leave it to me. Is there anything else I can do? If Adrian has deliberately lied about your trip to Norfolk then it should be a simple matter to tell the truth and repair the damage.'

'I don't think so. Circumstantial evidence is against me. I think any attempt at the truth would only add to the problem.'

'And you are back now to resume working?' Derek's face was impassive.

'Yes.' She nodded. There was a picture of Leanne in her mind, and her heart cried out for the child. Leanne had expected her to go to the cemetery. She glanced at her watch. If she were in Norfolk now they would be together, with a bunch of flowers for the grave.

Barbara went home at the usual time, sitting in her car in the traffic jam, only half aware of what was happening around her. Leaving Norfolk had been almost as traumatic as losing Charles. She had intruded into Jim Farrell's life and created havoc. Now she had been removed like a weed that had not really belonged.

She felt that she couldn't go on next day, but she went through the motions of her London life. Derek drove her into the office and she sat at her big desk as the routine of the day unfolded. Every now and again her eyes strayed to the telephone, and she kept telling herself that Jim was as close as the other end of the line. All she had to do was call his number and she would hear his voice. But she fought the temptation, and went to lunch in her favourite restaurant, refusing Adrian's offer to join them.

After lunch she went for a walk in Regent's Park, staying longer than she intended. How she wished Leanne was with her! The child would have loved feeding the birds and waterfowl. Tears prickled in her eyes and she returned to the office, lonely and aching, to find Derek waiting for her.

'You're late,' he greeted her tensely. 'I began to think you'd run off again!' He smiled to show that he was teasing, and he took her arm and led her to the door of her office, where he paused and looked down into her face. 'You have visitors. They're most anxious to see you. I've shown them into your office, and they're getting quite impatient.'

'I don't feel like seeing anyone,' she

responded dully. 'Get rid of them for me! You can handle anything that comes up during the next few days.'

'I admire your confidence in me.' He chuckled. 'I did talk to these two at great length but they won't be satisfied until they see you in person. They told me something about your life in Norfolk, and from what I've learned I believe you have a misunderstanding to settle.'

'Norfolk?' Barbara gasped, and jerked herself free of his hand to thrust open the door of her office. She strode into the room, eyes widening when she saw Leanne and Billy sitting at her desk. Leanne was eating crisps, her doll tucked under one arm, and Billy had a glass of lemonade. Billy looked a trifle sheepish, and got to his feet when he saw Barbara. She looked around quickly, hoping to see Jim as well, but the children were alone. She turned to look at Derek but he'd slipped away quietly.

'Barbie!' Leanne came across the office with arms outstretched and tears running down her cheeks.

Barbara opened her arms and swept the girl off her feet, burying her face in Leanne's hair. Leanne cried and clung to her.

'What on earth are you doing here?' Barbara demanded huskily.

'We ran away!' Leanne leaned back and peered at Barbara, smiling now despite the tears running down her cheeks.

'Oh dear!' Barbara smiled tenderly and kissed her. 'Let's dry those tears, shall we? Then we'll telephone your dad and let him know where you are.'

'Derek has already done that,' Billy said quietly, coming to stand at Barbara's side.

'I see.' Barbara reached out and patted his shoulder. 'And what did your dad have to say?'

'He's coming tomorrow to pick us up and take us back.' Billy shook his head. 'You've got a nice hotel here, Barbara! Is this the place I was coming to?'

'You still can, if you want to,' Barbara replied.

'I want to. Dad said this morning that if you did still offer me a place then I could come.'

'Very well. You'll find Derek outside. Why don't you go and talk to him? He'll show you around.'

Billy nodded and departed, and Barbara held Leanne's hand. She looked down at the girl. 'What are we going to do about you?' she asked.

'Can't I stay here with you? I could do odd jobs around the place.'

'You hated working in your father's hotel,' Barbara reminded her with a smile.

'But this would be different. I'd be with you.

Leanne looked up with eyes that were swimming with tears. 'Don't send me back, Barbie, please! Dad has fired Ruth! She's not coming back any more.'

'Poor Leanne!' Barbara kissed the girl's cheek. She recalled her own misery yesterday, when she had thought never to see this child again, and dropped to her knees and hugged her. 'I don't think we'll wait for your dad to come tomorrow to take you back,' she said softly. 'Would you like me to drive you home?'

'That would be better than having Dad come for us. But would you stay when you get there? You were happy with us, weren't you?'

'Yes, I was very happy!' Barbara considered for a moment, and then led Leanne to the desk. She called her secretary and asked for Derek to be located and directed back to her office. Then she called her home and Mrs Jameson replied.

'Pack a case for me,' she instructed. 'I'll be calling for it in about half an hour. Just enough things for a couple of days.'

'You're going to stay again!' Leanne clapped her hands.

'Your dad's hotel isn't the only one in the area,' Barbara said firmly. 'And I was supposed to be on holiday! I don't really know why I came back to

London, feeling as I do.'

Derek opened the door and looked in. Billy was with him.

'Derek,' Barbara said firmly. 'I'm taking the children back to their dad now, and I won't be in again this week. I'm going to stay on in Norfolk until I've settled the situation that came up there. I can't leave things as they are, with Leanne so upset. I've got to put matters right.'

'Well said!' Derek chuckled. 'I knew you would come to that decision and it's why I arranged this meeting. I needed to know exactly how you felt about things, and I thought the children would touch you. Are you in love with Jim, Mother? I know it's a personal question and you have every right to tell me to mind my own business. But just this once, please!'

She looked into his eyes, ready to deny it, and then glanced at Leanne and saw the unspoken plea upon the girl's tear-stained face.

'Yes,' she said quietly. 'Why shouldn't

I admit it? I do love Jim!'

'Then go along to my office and talk to him,' Derek retorted with a smile. 'He's waiting for you, if you should want to see him. He brought the children to London this morning. I talked to Adrian last night, made him see sense, and he spoke to Jim on the phone, explaining what had really happened. So go and get it sorted out. You know where my office is.'

Pushing open the door, Barbara peered inside. Jim was standing by the window, looking down on the busy London scene. He turned at the sound of the door and looked at her, a rueful smile on his lips. His face was taut and he looked as if he hadn't slept for a week. Barbara clasped her hands together, reliving the misery that had been her constant companion since leaving Norfolk.

'Jim!' she said softly, and went quickly to him.

'Barbara!' He opened his arms and she pushed herself into them. He clasped her to his chest and she closed her eyes.

Words were not necessary as their lips met. The misery melted away miraculously and Barbara's tension receded. This was her heart's desire — this man and his love.

'We'll talk later,' he whispered in her ear. 'I'll want to apologise and explain. But that can wait. I love you, Barbie, and that's really why I'm here.'

'And I love you, Jim! With all my heart!' She buried her face into his shoulder and her voice became muffled. 'We've got a date for Sunday, remember? The kids are keen to get aboard my boat.'

'And so am I!' He kissed her again. 'And there'll be lots of dates in future, I promise you.'

Barbara closed her eyes. She felt secure with his arms around her, safe in the knowledge that life was just beginning and the future lay waiting, filled with promise, hope and love . . .

Other titles in the Linford Romance Library:

WHERE DUTY LIES

Patricia Robins

The minute Charlotte sees Meridan Avebury at a wedding, it causes such a sudden feeling in her heart that she believes it must be love at first sight. But Meridan is already engaged to the beautiful Phillipa, who is dangerously ill. And while they don't deny their feelings for each other, Charlotte and Meridan are unwilling to take their own happiness at Phillipa's expense. However, Meridan becomes troubled by divided loyalties and struggles to find where duty really lies.